Between a Fox and a Hard Place

MARY FRAME

*To my mother in law, Debra Frame who was an avid reader
and all around kick-ass lady.
You are missed every day.*

She's determined to keep her family home. He won't let his friend down. Will conflicting interests shatter their chances of happily ever after?

Finley Fox refuses to give up her life's work. With her family's cabin rental business at risk of going under, the eldest of five has been laboring for years to care for the property, not to mention her now grown siblings. But when a New York billionaire makes a play for the ailing resort, Finley struggles to resist her attraction to the handsome man sent to secure the deal.

Archer Weston craves stability. With his best buddy since childhood in need of a favor, the lonely businessman heads to the mountains to convince the owner to sell. But his mission hits a hurdle when his heart melts in the presence of the hardworking, beautiful woman.

With debt and sibling drama piling high, Finley fears that leaning on her irresistible guest for support could end in her own heartbreak. But as their relationship grows and intensifies, Archer is caught between his long-term loyalty and his one shot at finding his forever...

Can this unexpected couple keep both their dreams alive?

Preface

Dear reader,

This book contains references to past deaths of a parent and young sibling by illness and/or accident. There is also a toxic relationship for one of the side characters and another side character struggling with alcohol abuse.

Thematically, this entire series is going to be a little more heart-wrenching than my other books, but there still is humor—because life is messy, but it's also funny.

I provide this warning so you can make an informed decision about whether or not to proceed. If you would rather read something more lighthearted, please check out the Imperfect Series or The Dorky Series if you haven't already!

Take care of yourself,
   <3
   Mary

CHAPTER

FINLEY

Happy hour. The unhappiest of all the hours.

"Where is he?" I stop on the other side of the bar, across from Veronica.

The restaurant is nearly empty. There are only a half dozen patrons in the whole place.

Jimmy and Paul are at the opposite end of the bar, grumbling at the hockey game on the flat-screen TV and sipping pints of amber liquid. Reed sits in a corner booth with Stacey. They both work in the county tax assessor's office—a number I have memorized at this point. He nods in my direction, and Stacey waves. I manage a distracted smile.

At a table near the front entrance, an unfamiliar man is nursing a half-full beer.

My eyes linger for a second on the stranger, mostly because it's odd to see an unfamiliar face mid-March, which is not anywhere near tourist season but also because *damn*. He has broad shoulders covered in a thick woolen blue flannel. His jawline is stubbled as if it hasn't seen a razor in three days. I've only caught a quick glimpse of his strong features and dark hair, but I liked what I saw. His nose is slightly too big for his face, and a small scar bisects one eyebrow, but the imperfections only make the whole package more compelling and also slightly dangerous. He's like a lumberjack: strong, beefy, possibly able to lift me with a single arm or exact vengeance on all my enemies.

If I wasn't exhausted, teeming with frustration, and ready to murder my little brother, I might be tempted to introduce myself. Except I'm currently wearing dirty overalls, muddy boots, and probably resting bitch face.

Might not be the best idea.

"Hey, Finley. He's out back. Rough week, huh?" Veronica winces in sympathy.

"Every week," I murmur.

"Thanks for coming so quick. I don't want to leave him out there to freeze his bits off when the sun sets." She shakes her head, her long silvery-gray hair swinging with the motion. Veronica went to high school with my dad. I often hoped he would date her, since she's a pretty sixtysomething woman, and she's single. But it wasn't meant to be.

I put my elbows on the scuffed wooden bar top and

clasp my hands together tight, resisting the urge to bang my head against the solid surface. "The bathtub again?"

She picks up a rag, wiping off the counter to my left. "It's his favorite resting place."

It's where he goes to pass out when he's next-level drunk.

I didn't want to deal with this today. Raccoons digging through our trash woke me up last night because Jacob didn't close the bin all the way. I spent my morning cleaning up the mess and then the afternoon digging drainage routes through freezing dirt—which is what I was doing when Veronica called. I haven't eaten since breakfast, and we have a few guests checked in today. I don't have time for any of this.

When I remain silent, she adds, "Do you need help getting him out?"

I blow out a breath. "No. I'll get him. You have customers. I just need a minute to prepare myself."

She grimaces and leans closer, lowering her voice. "This might be a bad time, but I'm not sure there will ever be a good one." She pauses, her gaze dipping to where my hands are still clenched before she meets my eyes. "Bernie was in here earlier with Estelle. They're selling."

My stomach drops. All the air is sucked out of the room. The world tilts. "No." My mouth forms the word, but no sound emerges.

She nods, tossing the bar rag out of sight below the

bar. "They want to retire next year, and they got an offer they couldn't refuse."

My back teeth clench. *Dammit.*

Bernie and Estelle have been our neighbors for as long as I've been alive—all thirty-two years.

If they've sold, this means every parcel around Fox Cottages, my family's property, has now been acquired by the evil overlord of doom.

My fists clench against the bar. "Damn him."

Veronica nods and clucks in sympathy. Everyone knows who *he* is—Oliver Nichols—some rich prick who's been flinging his lackeys in my direction every other month to pressure me into selling my land. Lord knows why he wants to buy rural property in East Bumfuck, New York, but I will fight it to the bitter end. I have to. My home is all I have left.

A familiar surge of fury and indignation flows through me along with a healthy dose of despair.

I might not have a choice soon. Especially if my damn brother keeps drinking our nonexistent profits.

Misery leaks into the air around me, and Veronica taps my hand with a gentle finger. "You need a little something?"

I glance over at the hottie lumberjack. *Yes. Yes, I do need something.*

But I'll settle for what's realistic.

"Yes. Please."

She grabs a glass from under the bar and pours a couple fingers of good bourbon into it. "This one's on the house. You enjoy that before you have to deal with that man out there. He was on one today." She chuckles.

He's on one every day. "Thanks, Veronica."

I'm grateful she called me. Even though I wish she would refuse Jacob service, I can't put her in that kind of awkward position.

I take a little sip of my drink, enjoying the burn.

After a minute, Veronica walks out from behind the bar, talking to the lumberjack in a murmur, giving him his check. I strain my ears to interpret his rumbling response, but it's too low for me to catch.

She heads back to the bar, and he tosses some bills on the table, leaving without so much as a glance in my direction.

I'm not sure if I should be disappointed that I'm invisible or relieved, considering my current appearance. There is no way I could snag a man that lickable without a few more hours of sleep and, at the very least, a half-hearted attempt at making myself presentable.

It's been a long time. I need to get laid.

Shoving the inconvenient thoughts of my neglected libido aside, I fling back the rest of the bourbon. I have bigger fish to fry. A brother to carry home. Or at least to the truck.

Once the heat from the drink has warmed my insides, and I feel less murdery, I gird my loins and head out the back door.

The air bites at my cheeks. The sun is descending, and the trees lining the property cast gloomy silhouettes.

About thirty feet away, resting in the corner of the property under a bony maple, sits an abandoned bathtub. Jacob's tawny-brown hair flicks in the breeze just above the lip of the tub.

I pick my way over the gravel and dead grass, skirting patches of snow lingering in the shadows, refusing to melt.

Perching on an old stump next to him, I wait.

He's been worse since his birthday—he just turned twenty-five. I wish it was your typical quarter-life crisis, but it's more than that.

His face is serene in slumber, not at all like that of a man who lost his twin sister at fifteen and hasn't fully recovered. He looks so young and so much like Aria it nearly takes my breath away. He has the same stubborn chin, aquiline nose, and thin lips they inherited from Dad.

A loud snore rips out of him, echoing around us.

Just perfect.

Time to wake up Sleeping Beauty.

I push on his shoulder.

The snore cuts off, and his eyes blink open. A sleepy grin takes over his face. "Hey, Fin."

"Hey, Jake."

His smile droops, his glazed eyes shuttering.

And then he's snoring again.

I smack his cheek. "Jacob. Wake up. We need to get to the truck, and I can't carry your heavy ass."

He groans.

I stand, lean over him, grab both of his hands, and yank him upward. He barely shifts. "C'mon."

He glares up at me. "I'm tired, Finley."

"Stop whining and get up. You can sleep when we get home."

"I don't want to go home." It's like he's five. All the thoughts about how sweet he looked as he slept die a quick and painful death.

"You can't sleep here."

"Why not?"

"Uh, because it's cold and uncomfortable and because I said so."

He moans again but at least makes a half-hearted effort to stand. It takes a few minutes of tugging and cajoling, but eventually, I've got him out of the tub and on his feet—wobbly feet—but progress is progress.

We shuffle around the side of the squat wood building, Jacob's arm around my neck.

I keep my gaze focused on our faded-green pickup truck while he drags his feet, his weight heavy across my back, his boots running into mine as he stumbles next to me.

We're crossing the entrance from the main road when he comes to an abrupt halt.

"Wait." The word slurs out of his mouth. Then he bends over, dragging me down with him, and throws up all over both our shoes. He sinks the rest of the way to the ground.

"Shit." *This is not happening.* I tug on him, holding my breath. "Jacob, get up."

He doesn't move, lying on the asphalt, a boneless lump of stank.

I glance around. At least there aren't any witnesses to this humiliation.

I grab his arm again and yank. "Come on, we have to move out of the way. We're blocking the entrance."

"It's fine." He relaxes even more against the hard ground. "Comfy here."

"It's not fine. Jacob. If you don't move your ass, I'm going to kick it."

No response.

"I'll tell the whole town about that time you microwaved your pee."

"No, you won't," he murmurs, eyes still shut.

I don't know whether to cry, scream, stomp him with my vomit-covered shoe, or all three.

A car pulls halfway into the lot, coming to a halt a few feet away—the tail end of the vehicle sticking out onto the main road.

"Just perfect," I mutter. "Jake, get up!" I yell directly into his ear.

He doesn't even flinch.

Standing, I turn toward the driver of the vehicle and lift my arms in the universal symbol for "I don't know."

They honk.

I lift my arms again. "You want to come out here and help me?" I call out, but their windows are rolled up, so I'm not sure if they can hear me or if they care.

They honk again.

Nope. They don't care.

Why me? Why can't I have a normal life where things go right once in a while instead of everything always going from bad to worse to absolute hell?

I'm so sick of the constant anxiety and tension and stress—I don't think I can take it anymore.

As if summoned by my defeatist thoughts, another car pulls up behind the first, and they both start honking, one after the other, a chorus of impatience.

Hysterical laughter gurgles up and bursts out of me.

CHAPTER

Two

"Let me call you back." I stare out the windshield at the scene on the other side of the small parking lot.

His response is a click on the line and then dead air.

I grin down at my phone. I've always found Oliver's lack of basic politeness amusing. It's probably why our friendship has lasted this long—and at least half of why it started in the first place.

The smile turns into a wince when the man on the ground throws up—again.

Jacob Fox. He checked me in at Fox Cottages only a few hours ago. How did he get this drunk so quick?

The woman who has been half carrying, half supporting him on their laborious journey from behind the bar throws her head back and . . . is she laughing?

Surprise lifts my brows. This must be Finley Fox.

The car next to them honks. The one pulled up behind it honks too.

She's doing her damned best, wrenching on Jacob's arms in a futile attempt to drag him out of the way, but she's laughing so hard he's not budging. Not that she could do it on her own anyway. She's half his size.

Oliver had texted me a blurry photo of her, taken from a distance. Her mouth was partially open, eyes half closed. It had been taken by one of Oliver's buyers, someone he sent to approach her about selling the property. According to him, she had tried to run the poor guy over with her truck.

After that failure, Oliver had tried again, sending two more of his lackeys, but apparently Finley threatened them with a shotgun.

I slide out of my rental car. This isn't how I want to introduce myself to Finley Fox, but maybe I can work it to my advantage. If I come to her rescue, maybe I'll have a better shot than those who came before.

Besides, I can't leave her like this.

"Need a hand?" I call out as I approach.

In the fading light, I get a better look at Finley Fox.

Her hair is dark, pulled back into a thick braid. Her eyes are lighter, harder to make out, maybe hazel, with faint shadows curved underneath. Her clothes are grubby, she has vomit on her shoes, and her skin is stretched with fatigue. But there is something in the curve of her jaw, the stubbornness in her chin, the set of her shoulders that sucks me in. I can't look away.

"Oh, this is just perfect," she grinds out, her voice full of exasperation.

I halt a few feet away, schooling my expression into a blank mask.

Does she know who I am? That I'm here at Oliver's behest? How could she?

She continues before I can formulate any kind of response that won't result in being maimed, shunned, or told off.

"No, please." One hand flicks up and then flops down at her side. "Because this day hasn't been awful enough, having a hot lumbersnack witness my mortification is really topping it off."

Her words shoot a spark of surprise through me. "Did you just call me a . . . lumbersnack?" I ask, unable to keep the amazement from my voice.

I'm not a small-statured person. Most people find me somewhat intimidating at first. I've never been referred to as any kind of bite-size portion.

The person in the first car rolls down their window. "Can you get out of the way?"

"Mr. Morgan, is that you?" She squints at the vehicle. "Can't you see I've got a little issue here?" She gestures with both hands at Jacob. "Have some sympathy or get out and give me a hand."

"Sorry, Finley, but I need to go to the bathroom. My

high blood pressure meds make me have to piss every twenty minutes."

I wave at Mr. Morgan. "I've got this." I heft Jacob up until I've got him in my arms, bridal style.

Without missing a beat, Finley hustles in front of me, leading me over to a battered and ancient pickup truck, opening the passenger door.

I set him inside. She grabs a towel from the bed and flings it over him. Then she puts a dirty paint bucket on the floor between his legs.

"Not your first time, huh?"

"Nope." Her mouth is a thin line. "Thank you for your help." She shuts him inside then faces me. "Mister, um. . .?"

"Weston. Archer Weston." I stick out my hand and wince. I didn't mean to introduce myself like like I'm James Bond.

"Finley Fox." She shakes my hand quickly, her grip firm. Her head tilts, gaze narrowing on my face. "Archer is an unusual name. I know that name."

My heart skips a beat. It's not likely she would know my connection to Oliver, not unless she did some serious digging, but it isn't entirely out of the question either.

The divot between her brow relaxes. "You're staying in cabin four."

My shoulders ease. I nod to Jacob. "He checked me in earlier. He was a lot more sober then."

She rubs the side of her head. "Small miracles."

I shove my hands into my pockets. "I was heading back to my cabin, so I'm going your way, if you need help getting him inside."

She nods, a slow motion that includes a flicker of her gaze. Wait. Did she just check me out?

"That would be great. Thank you for your help." She pauses and then blows out a breath before speaking quickly. "And if we could forget about that whole thing where I called you a lumbersnack, I would appreciate it. If I had known you were a guest, I would never have compared you to"—her face scrunches in thought—"something both brawny and appetizing."

I bark out a laugh.

Finley Fox is not what I was expecting, not at all. Of course, her warm feelings toward me will change once she realizes who I am.

I should tell her why I'm here.

And yet.

She's smiling at me, a small, tired smile, and I can't summon myself to utter the words that will ruin this . . . whatever this is.

Then we've been smiling at each other for a few seconds longer than what should be comfortable. Turning away, I call out over my shoulder, "I'll follow you back."

As I drive down the winding two-lane road, an internal battle wages in my mind.

I'm going to tell her. As soon as we get back and I help her get Jacob into bed, I'll come clean. I can't pretend I'm some random good Samaritan. I have to tell her the truth, right?

But if I don't tell her, then maybe she'll let down her guard, and I can ask her questions. It might be the only chance I have to figure out what's keeping her from selling.

Within a few minutes, we turn off onto the gravel drive. My headlights dip and weave over a few of the cabins interspersed with towering pines.

The property is extensive. The scattered cottages vary in shape and size. They're mostly A-frames, but there are a few square bungalows too, like the cabin I'm renting.

We turn left, curving up a slight rise toward the main house.

It's an eclectic structure, an odd mixture of architecture, as if different hands have been adding to it over the years and the result is something sort of charming and sort of misshapen.

The main office, where I checked in earlier, is in the front, basically a room connected to the residence by an interior door. Finley drives around, parking on the side next to an unattached garage.

Pulling up beside her truck, I take a few deep breaths.

I don't want to ruin her night—more than it has

been already—but waiting too long will make the repercussions worse.

I'm going to tell her. It's the right thing to do.

It's settled. Resolute, I get out of the car.

CHAPTER

Three

Finley

I flick Jacob on the cheek, leaning over him in the open passenger door. He snored the entire drive home. "Wake up, numbnuts."

His head rolls away, and he swipes a hand up, attempting to deter me. "Stop, Fin." His eyes are closed, his words thick with sleep.

Footsteps approach, and Archer appears next to me. "Finley, I—" he clears his throat.

I meet his gaze.

His eyes are dark and intense, surrounded by thick lashes that should be criminal on a man who's already hot enough to melt the frozen pond over the hill with just a smoldering look.

He stares at me for a few long seconds.

Jacob's arm flails up between us, reaching for nothing. "I gotta take a piss."

Archer steps closer. "Right. I-I've got him." And like I wished on a genie and summoned the hottest, most helpful and capable man I could wish for, he tugs on Jacob to get him out of the seat and hefts him into his arms like it's no big deal and he manhandles people all the time.

I scuttle ahead of him, leading the way up and through the side door and into the house. The sink is full of dishes. There's an open box of Cheez-Its on the counter, and the trash can is overflowing.

This is so embarrassing. My skin prickles with heat.

I pick up the pace through the living room and up the creaky wooden stairs to the second floor.

We head down the long hallway that leads to the back bedrooms. The photographs lining the walls are dusty. The floors need sweeping.

I've never stopped to consider the faded wallpaper and outdated wood paneling lining most of the interior. It's all been here since I was a kid, and I haven't had time or money to change it. All our profits go toward maintaining the cabins and keeping the business puttering along.

Archer and I stand outside the door, waiting, while Jacob fumbles in the bathroom. I hope he doesn't pass out and hit his head in there.

Finally, Jacob finishes, and I help Archer set him on

the messy bed, his feet hanging over the side so I can get his dirty shoes and pants off.

"I'll be just a second," I say.

He exits the room with a short nod, his footsteps receding down the hall.

I tug off Jacob's boots with a wince and then his dirty pants, throwing them in the full hamper in the corner. At least there's a clear path to the bathroom.

"What am I going to do with you?" I lift his legs to the bed and cover him with the old navy-blue comforter he's had since high school.

Archer is standing a few feet away, down the hall, his hands tucked into his pockets, gazing at the array of photos.

"It's a lot to take in at once," I say in a low voice, shutting Jacob's door. "We used to joke that Dad should have been a professional photographer."

"You have a big family."

I nod. I don't want to talk about my family. "Do you want a drink or something?" My voice is pitched too high, exposing the nerves racing through me.

I want him to say yes.

I want him to say no.

I want to take off all my clothes and fling myself at him as if I'm young and worry free and not an exhausted thirty-plus woman who feels fifty and is still raising her grown-ass brother.

He hesitates.

My bravado falters. I can't do this. *I can't.* I don't

even know him. Not to mention the ethical ramifications. I've never propositioned a guest. I've never been tempted until now.

My heart sinks. He's going to say no. It's written in the tightening of his eyes, the slight downturn of his lips.

Probably for the best, I console myself.

He swallows. "Sure." His brows lift, and he stares at me, a bit dazed, like he's as surprised as I am that he agreed.

I glance down at my dirty clothes. First things first. I stink. "There are beers in the fridge. Will you grab a couple? I can meet you on the front porch in a minute. There's a heater out there and blankets on the porch swing. It's really quiet, and we won't wake Sleeping Beauty." I clear my throat. "I need to freshen up real quick."

He stares at me for a long second and then gives a clipped nod. "Okay."

As soon as he turns away, I bolt down the hall to my room.

Whipping my clothes off like a whirling dervish, I race across the hall to the bathroom to rinse off—no way am I doing anything, even having a simple conversation with someone, until I've had a chance to disinfect.

I take a brief second to stare at myself in the mirror. No makeup, puffy eyes, messy hair . . . No one in their right mind would find this attractive. "What are you doing, Finley?"

I summon my courage. I'm taking a little moment for myself. That's what I'm doing. Don't I deserve it? A little bit of fun? A little bit of mindless pleasure? All I ever think about is this place and Jacob and my sisters and family and responsibilities. Haven't I earned this, just for one night? I will *not* feel guilty about grabbing a little slice of joy when it presents itself.

There's no guarantee anything will happen anyway. If he leaves and I end up rejected and alone, it's fine. It's not like I'll ever see him again.

If my life is going to continue to circle the drain, I might as well try to have a little fun on the way down, as long as no one gets hurt.

Bolstered by the thoughts, I throw on my favorite daisy-covered long-sleeved button-up, black yoga pants, and thick wool socks and head out to the front patio.

"Thank you for everything," I tell Archer a few minutes later.

We're sitting next to each other on the porch swing, beers in hand. I'm wrapped in one of the fleece blankets we keep out here for chilly nights, and Archer has one spread over his lap. The heater hums a few feet in front of us.

I breathe in the scent of pine and dirt and home. This is where I usually come to unwind after long days. Relaxing right now is impossible. I'm too conscious of the man beside me, the squareness of his jaw, the way the fabric of his flannel hugs his bicep, his hip only inches from mine.

He nods. "No problem. I'm happy to help."

Oddly enough, he sounds like he means it.

"It's nice out here," he says after a pause. "Quiet."

I stare down the gravel drive in front of us, leading into shadowy blackness. Beyond the porch, the night is dark and bracing, but we're sitting in a faintly glowing circle, our faces periodically brushed with threads of warmth.

"The heater helps." We both stare at it. "And the blankets," I add.

A stilted, tense silence builds between us, brick by brick.

"I should tell you why I'm in town. I—"

"No. I don't want to know where you're from or why you're here."

He turns in the seat to face me, thick brows lifted. "You don't?"

"I don't want to make small talk." The words are thrown out like a gauntlet between us, knocking the wall down.

He stares at me, unblinking.

I take his beer from his loose-fingered grip and put both bottles on the ground.

Then I face him. "I want you."

His entire frame goes rock still. My gaze trails over the stiff line of his broad shoulders before snapping back to his face and getting caught in his watchful gaze.

Words pour out of my mouth and into the stone-cold silence. "Sorry to be so forward, but I've had a shitty day, a shitty decade, actually, and you're here, and I find you incredibly attractive. This doesn't happen to me often." I tear my gaze from his to stare at my hands, clenching in my lap. "What do you think?" I force myself to look back at him.

He sits motionless, body tense, expression blank.

If he says no, I might run over the hill and throw myself into the frozen pond.

Jesus, he's going to say no. I need to up my seduction game. Bluntly asking for a night of shameless pleasure when I have no makeup on, haven't slept a full night in a decade, and just got puked on might not be the best look for me.

But then he speaks. "I think you're beautiful, but—" The masks slips, and the raw desire on his face sends a flurry of heated anticipation winging through my belly.

It's that flash of longing, quickly shuttered, that feeds my wavering courage.

I lean over and press my mouth against his.

His tense posture becomes even more rigid.

What the hell am I doing?

Throwing myself at a customer like a desperate loser, that's what I'm doing.

When you've hit rock bottom, I guess there's nothing more to fear.

I taste the surprise on his lips, but it's a fleeting flavor, segueing quickly into demand—hungry and urgent. He takes control, and I relinquish it willingly. His hands slide around my waist, and we twist closer together on the seat, the blankets sliding down, pooling around our hips. The pressure of his mouth, his tongue, his taste scrambles my brain, and my hormones take control.

I slide my hands up into his hair, tugging on the silky strands. His tongue is seeking, tender, claiming.

Wait a minute. Reality throws up a hand. No way a man this hot and good at kissing is single.

I pull back, and he gets one million brownie points for immediately releasing me.

We're both panting. I have to catch my breath before I can speak.

"Are you married?"

"No." His answer is immediate. If he's surprised by the abrupt question, the only sign is a couple of blinks.

"Girlfriend?"

"No."

I home in on his expression, trying to discern if he's telling the truth.

"Are you dating someone casually but it could be

construed as possibly serious in the near or not-so-near future?"

He's chuckling before I even finish the question. "No."

"Thank the heavens." I sigh in relief.

His hand finds mine, linking his fingers through mine, a gesture that's intimate and more tender than I would have expected after that blistering kiss.

"My work doesn't allow much time for socializing. I travel a lot. I don't date. Not in a while, anyway." He winces then opens his mouth and closes it again. His gaze dips down to the seat between us, where his hand still grips mine. "And about that, my work is, I—"

"No." I place a finger on his lips, and all of my worries and thoughts flee, heat spreading through me. His mouth is pink and full and soft and a total contrast to the hard lines of the rest of him. "I don't want to know where you are from or what you do. I don't want to give in to urges to stalk you and show up on your doorstep some lonely night months from now. Honestly, it's for your own protection."

He chuckles against my finger, a low, deep, throaty sound that spreads fire up my arm and through my chest, stretching down my limbs.

I remove my finger and replace it with my mouth.

He nips at my bottom lip, and I moan into his mouth.

I need to get closer.

Kicking both blankets to the ground, I shift on the

bench seat, twisting to slide onto his lap, my knees straddling his hips.

His hands slip to my sides, his big, warm fingers gripping my waist. His mouth is insistent, his tongue sliding against mine, probing and seeking.

I want more. I need more. More of his skin, more of his touch on me.

I reach for one of his hands and guide it up, covering my breast. He pulls back slightly. His pupils are dilated, his breathing quick and labored.

"Wait." He draws air in deeper and releases it. His hand clenches on my waist, pulling me closer even as he's shaking his head. "Jesus. Finley. I don't want to take advantage of you." His eyes search mine, filled with desire, but doubts lurk in the recesses of his gaze.

I swivel my hips against the unmistakable erection pressing up in his jeans. "You can't if I want it. Please. Exploit me."

CHAPTER
Four

Archer

I should have said no.

No to everything, starting with the drinks. It should have been easy. "No, thanks, and good night." Five words.

But I couldn't. Finley was staring at me with those big, luminous eyes, honest and nervous but doing it anyway. I liked her courage in asking for what she wanted without shame or preamble.

Saying *no* was an impossibility, and not just because it's been almost a year since I've been with a woman.

It's her. There's something about Finley that's alluring, an innate honesty and sense of humor that I'm not sure I've ever encountered before. All I know is that

I've never been so drawn, so attracted to a woman so quickly in my life.

And now . . . she leans back in my lap far enough to reach up and slip one button out of its mooring. Then another. And another. The beat of my heart increases in tempo with each detachment. Little white daisies pepper the dark top. I might get an erection every time I come across one of those little flowers for the rest of my life.

I stare, transfixed at the sight of her bare skin appearing one slow fastening at a time.

My mouth goes dry when she reaches the middle of her chest then moves down more.

She's not wearing a bra.

My heart stops in my chest and then resumes beating as she continues her slow progress. One. Two. Three.

My hands move without conscious thought, pushing the thin fabric back, over and down her shoulders.

She's completely bared to my probing gaze, nothing in the way, nothing to hide the most perfect, most exquisite breasts I've ever seen in my life.

"You should never wear clothes," I whisper.

She laughs, a sultry sound that I barely register over the roaring in my ears.

Every noble thought that was flashing through my head a second ago—how this is a bad idea, how I need to tell her why I'm really here before I let this go on any longer—all of it goes flying out into the cold night as the blood in my body rushes southward.

The world recedes. All that exists is this flawless woman in my arms and a roaring in my ears.

"Archer. Touch me." The words are whispered, simple, and yet so erotic that just the sight of her and those three words have the potency to push me right over the edge.

The strength of my physical reaction should be alarming, but I'm too turned on to care.

Her hips flex against mine, seeking the hard ridge of my arousal, her head tilting back.

I run my hand up her back to her hair flowing in long waves around her shoulders. Grasping the back of her neck, I direct her toward me to taste her mouth again. My free hand glides up the front of her body, but I stop on the soft skin under her breast.

She groans. "Touch me. Please."

With deliberate care, I cover her with my hand then trace my thumb around her nipple in a slow circle.

She breaks our kiss, moaning again, her hips moving erratically.

My erection pushes against the zipper of my jeans, begging for relief. I take a few quick seconds to undo my pants, tugging everything down far enough so that when Finley presses against me again, the only thing separating our bodies is her thin yoga pants.

Our gazes clash as we connect.

"Yes." The sound is hissed through her teeth.

I capture it with my lips, trailing a line from her mouth to her jaw then her neck, nipping and licking.

My hands reach up, cupping her breasts. She arches, stretching toward me. I duck my head down to take one nipple into my mouth, sucking gently.

Her hips falter, her mouth falling open as desperate, needy sounds emerge, sounds that drive me closer and closer to an inevitable breaking point.

Her hands grasp my head, holding me in place while she seeks her release. I tease and pluck at her breasts, using my mouth, my hands, nipping and sucking. Her movements become increasingly frantic.

She shudders and gasps, calling out my name into the night air.

Satisfaction pulses through me at her release, the sensation beating along in time with my rapid heart.

Her body slumps against me, all warm, sated, sweet-smelling flesh, and even though my erection is pounding with need, the moment is too blissful to disturb. I hold her, brushing my lips against the top of her head. I take a moment to breathe and enjoy the quiet, cool air and the slight weight of the relaxed woman in my arms.

"Take me to bed." Her voice is a sexy, raspy promise of mutual pleasure.

Every cell in my body tingles with desire. I'm on fire with want, with yearning for everything that sleepy, sultry voice promises. I'm hard as a rock. I want nothing more than to do exactly as she suggests and spend the rest of the night sating our urges, exploring every curve and corner of her body. The craving is overwhelming.

A thread of integrity reaches up and smacks me in the face. I can't. Not without telling her the truth. *Maybe it won't matter*, a naïve, drunk-on-arousal voice says.

"Finley." My arms tighten around her, a bigger instinct conscious of the fact that this might be the last time she's in them willingly. I nuzzle into her neck, inhaling her scent. She smells like soap and sweet arousal. "I'm here because of Oliver Nichols."

Her slow and easy breaths stutter to a stop. Her body grows tense in my lap, all the lethargic pleasure being erased one stiff limb at a time.

Before I can explain or say anything to excuse my behavior, she slides off me. I follow her movements as she picks up her shirt, covering herself while she pads to the door, the movement all but breaking my heart.

She doesn't slam inside like I expect. Instead, she shuts the door with a gentle click, then the lock slides into place, deliberate and quiet. It might as well be a hammer blow.

I take a deep breath and release it slowly, trying to calm my racing heart. I need to leave. She might be in there grabbing a gun right now, but *hell*. Images of the last half hour flash through my mind. I can't think straight.

The way she looked at me when she delivered her

proposition—direct, daring, and so incredibly attractive. The feel of her body, the responsiveness, the unrestrained passion . . . I squeeze my eyes shut and shake my head as if it will dislodge the images pounding inside.

I keep breathing, in and out, calming my body.

After a few long minutes, I stand, stopping for a second outside her door. What is she thinking? What is she going to do tomorrow when I don't leave as she expects? I don't think she'll actually shoot me or run me over. What would she do if I knocked? If I tried to explain . . . but how?

I jog down the porch steps to my car. I should have told her.

A minute later, I park outside my dark cabin and head up the steps.

Music floats on the breeze from the bungalow next door, along with voices and laughter. There's a couple staying there. I ran into them earlier when I checked in. The sounds of their merriment are a stark contrast to the isolation surrounding me like a frozen cloak.

Once I'm inside with the door shut behind me, the silent darkness threatens to swallow me.

I flick on the lights to reveal the open floor plan, kitchenette with breakfast bar, and two still-made queen beds.

I make my way to the bathroom to splash cold water on my face. Anything to cool me down. The last hour was like a fever dream.

I dry my face and hands on a white hand towel hanging to the side of the pedestal sink and stare at myself in the round mirror.

"What were you thinking?"

I don't answer.

My gaze moves to the clawfoot antique tub, the little seashell-shaped soap, and the mini shampoo bottles wrapped in vintage-style labels.

It's apparent they're doing what they can to capitalize on the old-school charm of the whole place, but it doesn't seem like it's enough.

My cell rings, blaring in the stark quiet, and I nearly jump out of my skin.

I pull my phone from my pocket. Oliver.

That's one surefire way to put a damper on a raging erection.

I told him I would call him back, and that was—I check the time—some hours before my world got rocked on its axis.

"Hello?" I exit the bathroom, sitting on the edge of one of the beds and toeing off my shoes.

"Any progress? Have you talked to the fiend? Why didn't you call me back?"

Talked to her? I've had my mouth on her. Pressed my cock against her heat. The shrinking arousal comes roaring back to life.

Not now, I mouth down to my lap.

"No. Yes. Sorry. I was . . . distracted." If distracted can be another word for "filled with raging lust."

"So, you made first contact and you're still alive. Good. I knew you would be the person for this job. How long until we make the sale?"

I stand up and pace. "I don't know yet. It might take longer than you want, and I need you to be prepared for that."

"What have you found out?"

I hesitate. Talking about Finley to Oliver feels a lot like betrayal, but why would that be? Oliver is one of the closest friends I have, the closest thing to family, such as it is. And despite the intimacy of our time tonight, I've known Finley for less than a handful of hours. I came here with the sole intention of convincing her to sell, even if that means digging into her life, needling out secrets, discovering her price. Everyone has one.

Finley and I have unmistakable physical chemistry, but we don't know each other. She certainly hates me now. It shouldn't feel shameful. This is what I do. It's not a bad thing. I make people happy, eventually. I'm not trying to hurt her.

I rub my chest, where a sudden ache throbs. "I haven't learned much. This place needs a lot of work, and by all accounts, she's doing almost everything on her own. Probably bleeding money."

"Tell me something I don't know."

"Despite the fact that this place is sucking her dry, monetarily and physically, this won't be easy. You know that. I'm going to need time to figure out how to offer her a deal she can't refuse."

I already knew getting her to sell would be difficult based on Oliver's prior attempts. But after meeting her and seeing the array of family photos . . . this isn't just her property and business. People fight to the bitter end for their homes, for their families. If I had a family or a home, I would too.

"I trust you will find a way. It's why I called in the favor."

I'm a fixer, a problem solver, the person who can take the worst businesses in the world and turn them into a moneymakers. It's a gift. Solving problems is something I've done my entire life, and I've had my share of problems. If Oliver understood empathy, he wouldn't have called me in on this, or he would be issuing warnings to not get too involved, to harm instead of help. But I don't think he's capable of comprehending those types of motivations, so he assumes I'll follow his orders to the letter. After meeting Finley though . . . I'm not sure it's possible.

"You know what this means to me," Oliver continues, his voice low. "It should be important to you too."

"It is. I'll work on it. It might take more time than you want, but you're going to have to deal with it." There. That will give me time, at least, to figure something out.

"What does Nora have to say about that? Doesn't

she need you for whatever commerce you're currently involved in?"

I chuckle. "Nora never needs anything. She's ten times smarter than both of us. She can handle things without me. Think you can do the same?"

"Of course," he clips out.

I smile. "And I don't want you calling me every day and harassing me about what's going on. I'll call you when I have information. Deal?"

"You're a real pain in my ass, Weston."

My smile turns into a grin. "I love you too, baby."

He hangs up without another word, and I laugh, but the humor dies quickly when my thoughts turn back to Finley.

I have to convince her to sell to Oliver somehow and also convince her to not murder me in my sleep for pleasuring her on her porch before abruptly informing her of my true intentions.

Thinking about her is a bad idea. My blood heats. Again. *Jesus.* It's as if I'm fourteen instead of thirty-four.

I go outside, following the wraparound porch to the darkness in back. I lean my elbows against the railing, facing the woods, letting the cold air cool down my body.

The property is perfect for what Oliver has in mind. There's enough acreage to create additional buildings, especially since he's purchased surrounding parcels.

The existing cabins can be renovated or completely rebuilt if needed.

I owe him this, and that means I need ideas. I need to get Finley to sell. Everyone has a price. There is always a path. It's just a matter of figuring out what the cost is, and that doesn't necessarily have a dollar amount. This place is falling apart around her. It has to be more of a burden than anything else. There has to be something she wants more than retaining ownership of this sinking ship.

I stay outside for long minutes, and eventually, my vision adjusts to the dim light.

Earlier in the day, when I first arrived and made a cursory exploration, she had been down by one of the cabins, digging. At least, I assume it was her, since the figure I had glimpsed from a distance was a woman wearing overalls.

There's a dip in the grade in the rear, suggesting potential water buildup. Someone's been digging trenches, clearly attempting to divert the flow, with little success.

I could fix it. I could help her.

I need to spend more time with her too. The thought of doing something active, something that will make her life a little easier, is appealing, and I don't want to examine that urge too closely. My mind latches onto the idea in favor of the lingering guilt.

One thing is abundantly clear: she can't sustain this

place alone. From what I've seen so far, she's been trying her damnedest, but it's not enough.

I've learned how to give people exactly what they need, even if it's not what they think they want.

She's going to be over here first thing in the morning to either kick my ass out or attempt to maim me or both.

I need to make sure she changes her mind and allows me to stay.

And I know just how to do it.

I smile into the darkness.

CHAPTER

Five

FINLEY

I wake up before the sun with a pounding head and a foul temper. I barely slept, my mind rolling over and over the events of the prior evening, my emotions pivoting between pure fury, acute embarrassment, and unwanted arousal.

I'm groggy and exhausted and not thinking clearly. On autopilot, I go through the familiar motions of getting dressed, heading to the office, and booting up the computer to check for any reservations or emails that may have come in overnight, all the while stewing over Archer and the fact that he works for . . . *him.*

I don't think it was Satan's plan to send in a seducer to convince me to sell. Reflecting on the events of the prior evening, knowing what I know now, Archer was hesitant to stay. The hesitation, the way he didn't push me into anything, the way he tried to tell me a couple of times about his work, the way he stopped to make sure I really wanted to go on. I basically had to jump on him, and oh, holy hell, the shame of that now.

Even if he tried to tell me, it doesn't matter. My blood is still boiling. He should have made more of an effort before I straddled his lap.

My fingers jab with extra emphasis at the keyboard as I pull up his reservation, like each angry punch of my finger is whacking him right in the face.

He *did* only reserve cabin four for one night, but obviously, he intends to stay longer. Dammit. He's here to convince me to sell, and that's not happening ever, let alone within a twenty-four-hour period.

How dare he. How dare he come here, all hot and built and kind and . . . and helpful, and turn out to be one of those pretentious fucknuggets. What a jerk.

Except he wasn't a jerk. The fact that he stopped everything before we could get to the next level, he did the right thing—eventually. And I can't even blame him for not stopping me sooner, considering I crawled into his lap and—can I die now?

I wilt, dropping my head down to the table. I consider banging my head against the desk, but I already have a headache.

He could have said nothing. He could have taken me to bed and done everything I wanted and relieved his not-so-little problem and then used my horniness against me. Isn't that how these people work?

My face burns with shame.

I can't believe I propositioned a complete stranger —a paying customer and an evil overlord—and then kissed him.

The incoming message box dings, and I sit up and toggle over to my personal emails.

Reed. I click on it even though I would rather run away and deal with anything else. Even Archer.

Hey, Fin, we need to talk. I saw you at Veronica's yesterday, but I was with Stacey and I didn't want to chat in front of her. Call me.

My stomach swirls with anxiety.

Reed works for the tax assessor's office, and he's my ex-boyfriend.

We're past due on property taxes. He's guided me on how to challenge the assessment and has been working from the inside to defer the payments for as long as he legally could.

I've always known he couldn't help me forever, but I continue to do my best to postpone the inevitable. Something will work out. It always does, right?

I thought I needed a little more time to make ends meet, but there is no end. It's just a black hole of money being pushed into this place. Tension and worry twine together to form a knot in my gut.

I delete Reed's email and avert my focus to the

issue at hand. Anger is a much easier emotion to grapple with than fear, stress, and anxiety.

Archer. I've got to get rid of Archer. No problem. I'll go over there right now and evict his ass. His hot, muscular, succulent . . . *dammit*.

The door connecting the office to the main house creaks open, and Jacob sticks his head inside, dark sunglasses concealing his eyes.

"Hey."

"Good morning sunshine," I yell at him as loud as I can.

He winces, pressing fingers to the side of his head. "I have a headache."

"You don't say."

I have one too, and it has your name on it.

He slumps against the doorframe. "I think I'll stick to scut work today."

Typical. I don't want to fight. I'll harangue him, he'll get defensive, we'll argue, and he won't even accomplish the menial tasks he intends to complete. I have enough problems to deal with. It's easier to stick your head in the sand sometimes. It's the way our family works: pretend nothing is wrong even when it's all crumbling around us.

I proceed the emotionally healthy way: by changing the subject and grabbing my rifle.

"Oliver Fucking Nichols sent another one of his lackeys."

"Why does he—?" He stops short, gesturing to the

rifle in my hand. "You know that thing doesn't work. It's a replica."

"It's not to kill." I shift it in my hands. "It's to torment."

"Oh, good, save the murder for when you really mean it. You want breakfast?"

"Yeah. In a minute. I'll be back shortly."

He waves me off before heading toward the kitchen.

I throw on the jacket hanging on the back of my chair and then head out the front. I manage to hold onto my anger and righteous fury the entire march over. I will not be distracted by his big shoulders or his big hands that were thick and strong and yet tender, not to mention his big . . . *Stop it, Finley!*

His black SUV is still parked out front. I stomp up the steps, cross the narrow patio, and pound on the door.

No answer.

I bang again. "I know you're in there."

After a few tense seconds, I press my ear to the wood.

Silence.

No, wait. There is a sound. Some kind of scratching.

It's not coming from inside the cabin though.

I walk around the porch and turn in the direction of the noise.

There's Archer, the rat. He's down by cabin two, and he's—my mouth drops open.

He's *digging*?

I gape in stunned silence for a long minute as he fixes my haphazardly formed ditches, punching through the frozen dirt with the shovel as if it's as fine and soft as beach sand.

Every spring when the snow starts melting, the puddle outside cabin two gets bigger and closer. I've been meaning to fix it, but I haven't had time or resources.

I had someone take a look last year, and what I really need is a piece of equipment to grade the slope so the water will run away from the cabins, but I don't know how to drive a machine, and I can't afford it even if I could. So I've been digging by hand, but it's slow and hard work, and I've barely made a dent, and now . . .

He doesn't turn around as I approach, my footsteps muted by the sound of the metal scraping through the dirt in rhythmic thrusts.

His back is to me. I halt in my tracks, struck motionless by the twist of his body under the thin, long-sleeved shirt as he moves.

I tear my gaze away to check out his progress.

Don't ogle the enemy.

He's almost done. It's not perfect, but it will get us through for a few months, maybe even until next year.

I'm stunned and maybe a little turned on. The combination is enough to make me forget my bloodlust in favor of having my curiosity assuaged.

When my tongue unsticks from the roof of my mouth, I finally speak. "What are you doing?"

He turns around and eyes the weapon hanging loosely at my side before walking over to cabin two and resting the shovel back where I had left it against the wall.

He faces me, pulling off his gloves, running one free hand through his disheveled hair, and I do my damnedest to not notice the broadness of his shoulders, the tapered waist, the long legs wrapped in messy jeans.

I fidget, suddenly conscious of my old, frumpy jeans and ratty jacket, forcing myself to meet his gaze.

"Finishing up the work on your drainage issue over here." He nods toward the channels he's dug up.

"Why? Why are you fixing it?"

He rubs his bristled jaw. "Because I don't want you to shoot me?"

I frown down at the ground. I should not be disappointed he wasn't encouraged into manual labor because of my magical boobs.

"Is that the only reason?"

One corner of his mouth quirks up. "And I want you to let me stay a little while."

Here it is. My jaw clenches. "Why would I do that?"

He shrugs. "Because you need my help. I know how to fix things."

"No." Anger grinds through me. I move closer, my hand clenching around my gun. "No way. You want to fix it up so that dickwhistle Oliver Nichols can buy it out from under me."

He shakes his head. "It's not about that. Not entirely. I sincerely want to help you."

Confusion coils with the fury. "Why? If you're here for Oliver, then you want me to sell. You don't care about me. Why would you?"

His head tilts back slightly, then he shrugs. "I understand why you don't believe me. You don't have to trust me. But I won't do anything to force you off your land. How could I? You can run me out of here any time you want." He gestures to the inoperable weapon dangling at my side. "What I can do is keep Oliver off your back for a few weeks and fix up some things around here. Can you afford to turn down free labor?"

I stare at him, baffled. This makes no sense. His words are not computing into logic in my mind. He's here to convince me to sell, but in the meantime, he wants to dig ditches and clean cabins?

"Why on earth would you do any of this? What are you getting out of it?"

He steps closer. "I get to tell Oliver you haven't tried to kill me and figure out something to make this whole situation mutually beneficial."

My shoulders tense. "I'm never selling."

He nods as if it doesn't bother him in the slightest. "I'm willing to accept that. All I'm asking is that you hear me out and let me stay for a few weeks."

"Why would I do that?"

"Because you have no reason not to. This is a win-win for you. If you decide not to sell, no hard feelings, and you get free labor in the meantime. I will continue to pay my nightly rent, so you're also getting a short-term customer and steady income, small as it is."

His straight talk is like an arrow shot right into the heart of the problems that I've been contending with for years.

He's right. But I don't like it. And what he's offering? It's almost too good to be true. "There's got to be some kind of catch."

"No catch. Just let me stay and don't kill me. We can make a deal. I'll do whatever menial tasks you want, but every night when we're done, talk to me and maybe answer some questions."

My defenses rise, preparing for battle. "Questions about what?"

"Purely business related."

I shift on my feet. "So let me get this straight. You're going to pay the rent on the cabin, and work for me—for free—and all you ask is that I answer some questions and listen to you blabber about why I should sell?" I stare at him, flabbergasted. "Something I've already made abundantly clear I don't intend to do."

His gaze stays fixed on mine. "That's right."

I release a huff of laughter. "This won't work like you think it will."

"Then you have nothing to lose and everything to gain. We can even put it in writing, and I'll sign it."

My tired mind sorts through any potential ramifications. This is like one of those crossroad demon deals where they give you what you want but sentence your soul to eternal damnation.

"What if there are questions I don't want to answer?"

"I won't force you to do anything that makes you uncomfortable. I'm not intending to ask anything embarrassing or personal. I know you find it hard to believe, but I truly want to help you."

I frown. "Why would you want to help me?"

"It's what I do. I'm a solvency expert."

I don't understand exactly what that means, but I don't want to ask. I don't want to know anything about him.

He could be lying, I guess, but it would be easy to verify his occupation with a quick internet search. Even though I want to hate him with every fiber of my being, I really only hate him with about a quarter of them. Maybe it's because I don't have to spend my morning digging or maybe it's my lonely, lonely lady parts, but there is something inherently capable and trustworthy about Archer.

Either he's telling the truth, or he's a sociopath.

Honestly, I'm not sure I'd care if he is a psycho as long as he's willing to clean toilets.

But there's one more thing I need to resolve between us.

I lift my chin. "You should have told me."

I don't have to explain what I'm referring to.

"You're right. I know, and I'm sorry."

I nod and glance down at his mud-splattered boots, unable to hold his steady gaze.

"But I can't be too sorry." His voice is a low rumble. "I wanted you too."

Startled, I lift my gaze to his. His face is inscrutable, unsmiling, serious.

"I still do," he adds.

Something flips low in my belly, a sensation I haven't experienced in a long time, if ever.

Attraction. Lust. Maybe respect for a worthy adversary.

I might be desperate and pathetic, and he's probably full of shit, but his words make me feel . . . they make me *feel*. He definitely wasn't faking that monster erection last night, and I haven't felt desirable in a long time. A really, really, really long time.

"Okay."

His brows lift in surprise.

He wants work? I can make that happen.

"We can meet at the main house after sunset for your"—I wave a hand—"interrogation or whatever. We'll meet on the por—in the office." I almost suggested the porch again, not wanting to have him in the house, but what a bad idea that would be. The location of the *incident*.

Clearly, my brain is malfunctioning due to lack of sleep and surplus of stress. Heat spreads through my cheeks.

This is just business.

He nods. "Sounds good."

"I'll bring you a list of chores. While you're waiting, you can get started by cleaning the outhouse. Some guests last week thought it was still usable." I grimace. "And they didn't quite make it in the hole."

He gapes at me in horrified disbelief.

I turn away to hide my chuckle. "I'm kidding. Lighten up, Archer," I call over my shoulder.

Archer

"What are you doing?"

I'm crouched behind a dryer, examining the thermal fuse.

Finley stands in the open doorway, glaring down at me, resembling an angry kitten in her faded jeans, a red flannel, and tan work boots.

I'm not sure what's more amusing: Finley taking great pleasure in ordering me around, having me do menial and disgusting tasks for the past couple of days, or Finley getting more and more frustrated that I've been meeting her demands without complaint.

My current round of tasks has been washing all the sheets for cabins one through three in what Finley referred to as the laundry chalet, but it's really an old, windowless, and dusty shed with a few naked bulbs dotting the ceiling. There are three sets of washers and dryers, but one of the dryers is out of service, so I pushed it away from the wall to access the back panel.

I would love to be able to fix it, if only to get Finley's eyes to flash at me again.

"I think it's the thermal fuse. We just need to replace it."

Her hand grips the doorknob. "*We* do?"

"I'll keep you updated." I duck my head to hide my smile.

"Are you doing the chores in the order I gave them to you?"

"Yes. And I'm doing them in spite of the fact that you haven't lived up to your end of our bargain."

Her jaw is so tight it might break. I'm clearly exceeding her expectations if she's this pissed off. There are still a couple hours of sunshine left, and I've finished more than half the items on her list today, a list that has doubled every day.

The first night when I arrived at the main house to talk to her, Jacob told me she was sleeping. Last night, I asked two questions before Jacob came running in with an emergency C-section—which he tried to explain had something to do with their sectional sofa after Finley gave him a pointed and exasperated look. They don't have a sectional sofa, something she knows I'm aware of since I carried Jacob through their living room the other night.

"You fixed that backed-up toilet in seven?" She taps a foot on the concrete floor.

"Yep. The shower was draining slowly too. I used a snake to clean everything out."

I stand from my crouched position and push the dryer back against the wall, facing away from Finley.

"When I'm done with this, I'll start on the gutters." I turn to face her, and our eyes meet a beat later, after her gaze has dragged up from somewhere in the middle of my person.

I bite down on the urge to smile. "Were you just checking out my ass?"

Her mouth pops open then shuts. "Of course not." Her protest is overly loud in the confined space.

"You were too."

Her cheeks flush, and I release the grin that's been nudging at my mouth. It's irrepressible.

I expect her to fight me more or storm away. But she doesn't.

"Fine." She releases her vise grip on the doorknob and crosses her arms over her chest. "I was looking at your ass. I can't help it that you look like that. Maybe you should dress less provocatively." Her tone is accusatory.

I glance down at myself with a frown. "Less provocative than jeans and a dirty sweater?"

She nods emphatically. "You're just asking for it."

Before I can respond to that surprising comment, she exits with a huff and a flick of her braid.

Amusement spreads through me like a warm wave. The dryer buzzes, and I pull out the clean sheets, folding them into the hamper so I can take them back to the cabin.

We have undeniable chemistry, and I know she feels it too. I've been doing my best to keep everything professional. We've gone down that road, and she doesn't want anything further. I can't put her in an awkward position—again. She's already running herself ragged, which is why I haven't pressed for my time the past couple of nights.

I move laundry from the washer into the dryer and push the button, resting my hand on the top of the machine where it's warmest.

I've made it my life's work to help people who are struggling. Maybe I do that because of my upbringing and being the sole person my mother relied on from a young age, but this is . . . different somehow. This isn't my normal drive to help a business get back on its feet, earning the satisfaction from taking the most impossible case and giving it a chance, giving the owner hope.

I wasn't sent here to give her hope or to save this place. I was sent here to fulfill my duty to Oliver and get her to sell it to him. Then I'm leaving. Nora, my business partner, is going to need me sooner rather than later. I have a life to return to, a . . . well, I don't have a home per se, not since mom died. But I enjoy my job for the most part, although traveling so much has started to wear on me just a little.

I pick up the hamper and head out of the dark shed and into the early-spring day, squinting against the sun, the patches of snow still lingering on the ground casting up reflective light.

A trill of laughter coming from the main house catches my attention.

Jacob lobs a dirty snowball at Finley, and she retaliates by chucking a disposable coffee cup at him. He lurches out of the way, barely escaping getting knocked in the shoulder by the cup. It skips over the ground, spilling dark liquid all over the gravel drive.

"Finley!" Jacob's voice carries over the fifty or so feet between us. "That was almost full."

She throws her head back, her laughter bright and infectious.

My chest squeezes with some unquantifiable emotion.

Jacob's eyes cut to mine. Finley follows his gaze and twists in my direction.

Embarrassment flushes through me. I immediately turn away, heading toward the cabins to finish this round of chores.

It's because I've never had any type of family connection. That's why it impacts me. It's not because of my attraction to Finley.

Even though there's something about her that feels like home.

I shake my head in disbelief at my own thoughts.

What am I thinking? I barely know her, and she hates me. We have a deal, and I can't break it.

Which means I need to keep everything between us strictly business. I'm going to find a way to help her and appease Oliver, as impossible as it sounds.

But if she propositions me again, there's no way in hell I'm going to say no. I have morals, but I also know my limits, and when it comes to Finley Fox, I have a feeling I would give her whatever she wanted.

"How many employees do you bring on during the peak season?"

"We hire part-time help with cleaning and maintenance from June to August and then November through about mid-January." She rests her elbows on the desk, only partially covering a giant scratch marring the scuffed surface. "In the off-season, we have a couple of high schoolers that help run the office for volunteer hours and business experience, mostly on Saturdays."

I lean back and lift an ankle to the opposite knee.

So far, everything she's told me has been logical. She's doing everything she can to keep this place running. There's no conceivable way they could manage it year-round with only the two of them. They barely manage now, in the slow season, with only a few cabins in use. Payroll is the largest expense for most employers, so cutting that out wherever possible makes sense for her situation.

"How do you split the duties for the remainder of the year?"

"Jacob handles all the social media marketing. He checks people in and out and handles any concierge duties. He operates our website for online booking and adjusts our rates based on demand, answers emails, you know." She nods to the computer next to her.

I glance at the piece of equipment. It has to be at least ten years old, ancient as far as tech goes.

"He also cleans and helps with maintenance as needed. I do some of the simpler things with the computer, just in the mornings: responding to emails, checking for online bookings that come in, that sort of thing."

Because Jacob might be hungover. He disappears most afternoons before dinner and doesn't come back until dark.

"I keep track of income and expenses," Finley continues.

I nod, pointing my gaze to a basket of fake daisies at the corner of the desk, trying to think, which is diffi-cult to accomplish while looking directly at her. I like her appearance a little too much, her pouty lips, her stubborn chin, the way she can't hide her emotions. The silky strands of her dark hair and how it slipped through my fingers when we . . .

I shift in the seat.

Keep it professional.

We've been talking for a little bit, and to her credit, she's been answering all my questions, even if she hasn't smiled once. Maybe she figures she owes me since she's avoided me almost entirely the past couple of nights.

From what I've gathered so far, they were making ends meet until a few years ago—scraping by, really— and then some of the nearby resorts upgraded their facilities with new construction and better amenities, which shot their regular clientele list down to almost nothing.

They've done a decent job trying to market the old-school charm of the place, which helped some but not enough, and they don't have the funds for any serious transformations.

I'm still staring at the fake bouquet of daisies, but they only remind me of the other night and her daisy-covered top and what happened when I pushed that shirt off her shoulders.

I rub the back of my neck. "Have you ever thought about changing it up, like using the property to generate a different income stream entirely, other than renting out the cabins?"

She blows out a breath and fiddles with a paper-weight. "I have. I've researched a variety of additional business options, like adding a wedding venue, starting a pizza farm, beekeeping, a pumpkin patch, corn maze, storage, horse stables, ice skating rink, you name it."

"That's quite a list."

One shoulder bobs up and down. "I'm open to suggestions. You're still here, aren't you?"

"This is true." I lean forward in my seat, resting my forearms on the desk. "What would you do with an ice rink?"

Her head tilts to one side. "Teach classes. Or chore-ograph. I was—" She clears her throat. "I teach classes once a week over in Binghampton for extra cash." She waves a hand in dismissal. "But it doesn't matter. Every idea I've come up with requires capital and time that I don't have."

"What if you mortgaged the property—"

"That's already been done." She picks up the paper-weight again, a heavy bronze sculpture of a woman posing or something.

No. I stare at it with interest. It's a woman with one leg up behind her head and little ice skates on her feet.

She plops it down with a heavy clank and then picks up a pen, tapping it on the desk.

I hesitate. Following this trail of questioning might delve into something personal, but it would help me understand her position and how to best leverage it to make a deal with Oliver—to make one that would be to her advantage.

"When?"

She won't meet my eyes, gaze focused on the desk

between us. "Years ago. Dad did it. I didn't know until he passed, but he'd already taken money out against the property. More than once."

I sit back. "I see." This isn't good. If it's already mortgaged to the hilt, that means she has a monthly payment on top of everything else. No wonder she's sinking.

She swallows and drops the pen with a clatter. "It's bad. I know. But I still can't sell."

I nod. "I'm not asking you to." *Yet.* "Knowing the whole financial picture would be useful."

Her gaze narrows. "Useful for whom, exactly? I still don't understand your endgame here."

"I don't have an endgame."

She huffs in disbelief. "Everyone has an agenda. No one does something for nothing. You're here to help Oliver. He's your friend. Not me. Why should I trust you with anything?"

I open my mouth to respond, but my phone lights up, vibrating on the desktop between us.

It's Nora. Her picture appears on the screen, one she took of herself making a kissy face.

Finley's eyes dip down between us then shoot to the side.

"Sorry, just one sec." If I don't answer, she'll keep calling. "Hey, Nora. Can I call you back?"

She's silent for a beat. "What is this?" Her voice is full of disbelief. "You have something going on more important than me?"

"I know it's hard to believe. Something tells me your wounds will heal."

"Well, I'm slightly wounded but mostly skeptical." She laughs and then lets out a beleaguered sigh. "Fine. Call me when you're free."

We hang up, and I glance over at Finley.

Her brows are furrowed, her mouth set. "You said you were single," she says. Her voice is tinged with hurt, but that can't be right.

"I am single." I put my phone in my pocket. "Nora is my business partner."

Her jaw flexes as if she wants to comment further.

"And she's married. She's been with her wife, Jessica, since they were in high school."

She presses her lips together for a brief moment, and then her shoulders slump. "I'm sorry." Her eyes meet mine. "I shouldn't have jumped to conclusions. That wasn't fair."

"It's understandable. Don't worry about it." Surprise flickers through me at how easily she admitted fault and then apologized. Most people would rather die on hills of denial before admitting fault.

"Do you both work for Oliver?" she asks.

"No. Nora and I are co-owners of Lum-Weston Industries. Oliver is a friend. I owe him a favor, so here I am."

"Hm. It's a pretty big favor to take time from your life to spend in suffering."

"I'm not suffering."

"Then I guess I need to work you harder." One corner of her mouth tips up.

It's almost a smile but not quite.

"I guess you do."

She presses her lips together. "Nora is also a solvency expert?"

"Yes. We work together, but we have different strengths. She's brilliant. She speaks multiple languages, she can gather data like you wouldn't believe, but she's not as good with people. She has a hard time reading subtext or being sensitive to undercurrents. She's like a blunt force of nature."

We make a good team. I schmooze while she intimidates, which is ironic considering she's barely five feet tall.

"What does a solvency expert do, exactly?"

"We review businesses that are struggling for ways they can improve or turn a profit. Sometimes we buy them out ourselves and restructure them, depending on our capacity and their individual needs and goals."

I observe, communicate, get people to open up, research, then I fix all their problems.

"I know you find it hard to believe, but I enjoy making a difference in people's lives. Finding what will make them happy. I want to help you too. I just have to figure out how to do that and keep my promise to Oliver."

Her nose wrinkles with open skepticism. "Sounds impossible."

"Nothing is impossible."

Her brows lift. "If you solve my business's problems, I won't have a reason to sell to your friend."

I tilt my head. "There's always a solution. We just have to find the right one."

She frowns. "What does he want with my land, anyway? To turn it into ugly high-rise condos? Puppy farm? Slaughterhouse for adorable bunnies?"

I chuckle. "No. He wants to turn it into a kids' camp."

Her brows drop into a furrow. "Really?"

The front door bangs open. "Honey, I'm home," a feminine voice rings out.

A twentysomething dark-haired woman saunters in, smiling brightly. She looks a lot like Finley except her hair is a shade lighter, her eyes are wider, and her mouth is a little thinner. She's wearing dark leggings, giant furry boots that go nearly to her knees, and a tight neon-pink tank top, visible under a fur-lined coat.

She heaves an exaggerated sigh when she sees Finley at the desk. "Of course you're still working."

Finley gets up, blocking me from view, and hugs her. "You're back."

"Only for a few days." She cranes her neck to peek around Finley at me.

Finley steps to the side, hiding me again.

"There's a music festival in Florida next week." She

peeks over Finley's shoulder. "It's too cold up here this time of year for me to hang for too long." She ducks to one side. "But I was passing through and thought I would, um—" She fakes left then pops around Finley on the right, smiling brightly. "Aren't you going to introduce me to your friend?" she asks without removing her gaze from mine.

"He's not my—"

I stand, sticking my hand in her direction. "Archer Weston."

"Hey, Archer Weston." She drags out the syllables in my name and then rests her hand in mine briefly. "Taylor Fox."

"Archer Weston is not my friend. He's a guest here, and he's leaving." Finley not-so-subtly jerks her head toward the door.

Taylor's mouth pops open on a laugh. "Finley, don't be rude. Why are you hanging out in the office? Are you making the guests work now too? You really are a tyrannical dictator about this place." Taylor waves her off before turning back to me. "Are you staying for dinner, Archer? I love your name and your" —she eyes me up and down—"shirt."

She's grinning and Finley is glowering. None of this seems like it can end well, so I decide to make a neat escape.

"I wouldn't want to intrude on family time."

"It's no intrusion. I'm sure we can squeeze in one more person at the dinner table, right, Fin?" She shoots a look at Finley over her shoulder and then winks at me.

"I'm not sure I have enough food, actually," Finley grinds out. "I only planned for me and Jake, so adding you will require some finesse."

"She might be right. You look like you have a giant . . . appetite." Taylor's gaze pauses on my crotch.

Finley's face is a storm cloud.

Laughter tickles the back of my throat, but I manage to hold it back.

Taylor is a bit crude, sure, but somehow, it doesn't toe the line over into smarmy. She's got an angel-sweet face, and she's all lightness and humor and clearly doing her best to needle her sister.

"I should be going anyway." I'll put Finley out of her misery. "It's getting late." I edge around Taylor. "It was a pleasure to meet you."

"Oh, believe me, the pleasure is all mine."

I pass Finley on my way out and stop next to her, close enough to catch a glimpse of the flush on her skin where her top dips down into a V and get a whiff of her sugary scent.

"I'll see you tomorrow morning?" I ask in a low voice.

She gives me a clipped nod.

"I look forward to tomorrow's chore list."

Her lips twitch, but she doesn't smile.

I shut the front door behind me, and their voices seep out through the thin wood.

"What was that all about?" Taylor asks.

"What was what all about?" Finley's voice is an octave higher than normal.

"We need to talk about that hunk of man meat."

I grin into the night.

"There's nothing to tell. Let's go into the house."

Their voices fade further, but the teasing laughter lingers in my mind. A pang of loneliness slices through me.

I push off the door, jogging back to my cabin in the dark. The sting of her dismissal is minor compared to the nagging awareness of my status as an outsider.

I can't imagine what it would be like to have a large family. Or any family. What would it feel like to have people dropping by, to have a home to return to where you can tease and cajole and love?

My whole life, I've been mostly alone. But I've never felt this lonely.

FINLEY

"Nothing to tell, my ass." Taylor follows me, an annoying presence chirping at my back.

"Is he single? Are you sleeping with him?"

"What? No. It's none of your business, and why do you care?"

I flick off the office lights, and we go through the door that connects to the living room. "He is. And you are. And if you aren't, you want to." Her voice is accusatory as we enter the kitchen.

I stick my head inside the fridge, trying to ignore her, but it's like trying to ignore a bee buzzing next to my ear.

"You have a hot single man within spitting

distance, and you're not going for it? That's a waste of good man flesh. Someone should take advantage."

I root around for a drink, pushing aside a block of cheese and a bag of carrots. The only beverages in the fridge are expired oat milk and a few cans of soda. Damn Jacob. He's made it hard to keep booze anywhere in the house because it always disappears within a day.

I stand up and shut the fridge. "He's not a plaything that's only here for your amusement. No one is taking advantage of anyone." I won't mention the ogling or the flirting or the orgasm on the porch.

"Who's taking advantage?" Jacob enters from the side door.

Taylor shrieks and jumps on him. "Jakey!"

"Tay-Tay!"

He swoops her around, and they're both laughing and talking as if they didn't see each other last month and go through this same ridiculous routine.

I move to the sink, rinsing off a few dishes from breakfast and lunch and putting them in the washer.

Taylor comes and goes once or twice a month, usually only staying a night or two at the most. She lives in her VW bus and travels across the country, going wherever the wind takes her, working odd jobs and attending music festivals with a rowdy group of eclectic friends, ranging from hedge fund managers to C-list celebrities.

I love my sister. I'm happy when she's here, but Jacob is usually worse off when she leaves.

"How long are you staying?" Jake asks.

I dry my hands on a dishcloth and turn around, leaning back against the counter.

Taylor shrugs. "A day or two. There's a big show in Fort Lauderdale. Tortuga. Can't miss it. Although you have a guest here that might encourage me to stay longer." She winks at me.

"What are you talking about?" Jacob jumps up onto the counter next to Taylor, his legs swinging back and forth.

"Archer Weston."

Jacob scowls. "He's still here?" His eyes dart to mine.

I explain for Taylor's benefit. "I made a deal with him. He's going to help around the cabins for free, and all I have to do is answer a few questions."

Jacob's brows furrow. "How long did you say this deal is going to last?"

So I may have glossed over some of the finer points.

"Yeah, Finley, what kind of *arrangement* do you have with this guy?" Her tone goes dreamy. "He has a great aura."

"Taylor." I give her my best older-sibling-in-charge voice accompanied by a warning look.

She laughs. "C'mon, spill it, sis."

I blow out a breath, knowing she won't let me get

away with anything but the full explanation. "Archer is here because of Oliver Nichols."

Taylor's mouth pops open. "Oliver Nichols? Isn't he the guy who keeps making those huge offers on the property?"

I nod.

Jacob frowns at me. "You're not selling, right?"

"No. I'm not selling." My voice is firm, but inside, something quavers just a little bit. I might not have a choice soon, but I can't tell Jacob that.

His shoulders relax.

"Maybe you should consider it," Taylor says in a low voice.

Jacobs head snaps in her direction. "It's not going to happen."

"We're not selling," I agree. "It's pointless to even bring it up."

Taylor holds both hands up. "Sorry, sorry. I know, this is our home. I don't want to lose it either. It was just a suggestion."

"It's a stupid suggestion," Jacob mutters.

"Your face is stupid."

He grins at her. "We have almost the exact same face, so you're calling your own face stupid."

"Anyway," I cut in. "I've told him we aren't going anywhere, but he's offering to work and help out around the cabins, and I just have to answer questions about our business."

Taylor leans back against the counter next to Jake. "What kind of questions?"

"So far, it's standard stuff. What our busy season is, how many employees we hire." I think over our conversation. "I probably asked him more questions than he asked me." I shake my head. "I don't know. He might be crazy."

"Crazy hot." Taylor grins. "That scar on his eyebrow makes him look wicked, but like in a good way."

Jacob grimaces.

I sigh. "He offered free manual labor, and if all it costs me is a few conversations, we can't afford to turn it down."

Taylor sighs. "A hot guy who cleans and does chores. Seriously, what kind of thirst trap is he setting here?" She gasps and grabs Jacob's arm. "You should use this. Post pictures of him vacuuming and changing light bulbs and whatnot on your social media. Get him to take his shirt off too. I bet every single woman in a two-hundred-mile radius would book a weekend getaway. Probably some guys too."

It would have seemed like a good idea if the mere suggestion of strangers on the internet looking at Archer half naked hadn't sent a bolt of jealousy shooting through me. *Get it together, Finley. He's not yours to lust over and he never will be.*

Jacob gives her a weak shove with the back of his

hand. "What am I? Scrum under a rock? You could take my picture."

Taylor wrinkles her nose. "No way. You can't be considered attractive. You're my baby brother. Plus, you live here. We don't need anyone becoming stalkerish and trying to kill you or living in the walls or something."

I groan and cover my face. "I don't want to talk about people living in walls or anyone lusting over my little brother." I remove my hands. "What do you want for dinner?" I mentally evaluate the contents of our cupboards. "I can make grilled cheese and soup or something."

"You work too hard. No cooking tonight." Taylor claps her hands together. "Let's go get dinner at Veronica's. On me."

"I need to shower." I'm covered in dirt and crud, and I feel like mold and grime and dust all rolled together and made a filth baby.

"Okay, you take care of your little hygiene issue, and Jake and I can go and grab some food and bring it back. Then we can veg out and binge watch *The Tenth Kingdom*." She lifts her brows at me hopefully.

I smile at the name of an old, slightly ridiculous but charming miniseries from twenty-plus years ago that they used to watch over and over when they were kids.

"Sounds good to me. I could use a drink." Jake pushes off the counter and grabs the truck keys from the hook.

"Keep an eye on him," I tell Taylor in a low voice before she follows him out the side door.

She stops in the doorway. "Stop worrying so much."

"He's been drinking a lot."

She pats my shoulder. "He'll be fine. We'll be back in a flash." She gives me a quick hug and then disappears out the door after our brother.

I hope she's right.

An hour and a half later, I've showered and changed, and they've returned with the food—burgers from Veronica's, plus popcorn and M&Ms for extra snacking. I queue up the show and we eat, Taylor and I sitting on the old, worn couch in the living room while Jacob sprawls out on the recliner.

We've barely made it through the first episode when Jacob falls asleep and starts snoring louder than the TV.

"Poor guy, he must be exhausted. You running him ragged or what?"

"Taylor, he drank six beers and had how many shots while you were at Veronica's? It's not me."

She frowns over at him. "I don't know what he had. I wasn't paying much attention. But I'm sure it's just a phase. I drank too much when I was younger too."

I roll my head over on the sofa to give her a look. "He's a year younger than you."

One shoulder bounces up and down. "He's a boy.

They don't mature until forty-five—if you're lucky. He's basically twelve."

I sigh. "I hope it's a phase, but I'm worried about him." I want to unburden myself completely, but I hold back.

I'm not used to having frank conversations with my younger siblings because I've been more of a mother figure than an older sister.

Maybe Taylor is right, and it will all work itself out. But what if she isn't? Maybe there's nothing I can do, but I wish there was someone who could at least understand. Someone I could vent to that could just listen.

Taylor is older now, and maybe we've reached a point where I can share some of the load I've been shouldering. "Sometimes I feel like everything is falling apart."

"You worry too much." Then she pats my leg, like I'm the younger sibling and she used to change my dirty diapers instead of the other way around. "Everything always works out in the end. You don't have to know how; you just have to trust that it will." Her eyes scan over me, and she sits up straighter. "I know. You should let me give you a reading. The stars have been showing some weird things, but there's a shift coming for you." She taps her lips with a finger. "I can sense it."

I wave a hand at her and try not to roll my eyes too

hard. "I know, I know, it's a full moon, and Mercury is in Gatorade or whatever."

She laughs softly. "There she is. Don't go getting all serious on me, or I'll have to start calling you Mindy." Her tone is teasing, but the glint in her eyes tells me otherwise.

"Have you talked to her?"

She averts her gaze, looking ahead at the TV. "Not since Christmas."

She means the Christmas before last, more than a year ago. They got into some kind of fight or argument, but neither would say what it was about. There was a lot of bickering and sniping, and it was horrible and awkward.

Mindy and Taylor were never besties or anything but nothing as bad as this. They are about five years apart in age, Mindy being only a year younger than me. When we were kids, it was a big gap, but even as they've gotten older, their relationship has never improved. It's only gotten worse.

"What happened with you two, anyway?" I throw the question out there. I don't think she'll tell me, but I give it a go anyway.

She reaches over to the coffee table to grab the bowl of popcorn. "Nothing happened. We're just completely different people. I'm fun and she's not, and that's it. I don't want to talk about Mindy. Have you talked to Piper lately?"

I wince. "Sort of? You probably talk to her more

than I do. We've texted, but she never answers when I call, and I feel like she's ignoring me. But maybe I'm being paranoid. She's so busy all the time."

"We met up for coffee last month when I was going through California."

"Was Ben there?"

She picks through the popcorn bowl, hunting for the M&Ms. "I only saw him from a distance and just for a second. He dropped her off and then picked her up when we were done."

I take a deep breath and release it, trying to not stress about things I can't control. It's everything. I can't control anything.

"How was she?" I ask.

"She seemed okay. Too skinny." She nudges me with her elbow and puts the popcorn bowl in my lap. "Kind of like you."

I shove a few pieces into my mouth. "It's not by choice." I have no time to eat, and the time I have is spent doing manual labor.

"You need to enjoy your life rather than trying to control everything. Maybe you need a hot flannel-wearing businessman to take the edge off." She raises her brows suggestively.

I groan. "Not this again."

She laughs. "Tell me seriously what's going on with this Archer guy."

"There's nothing to tell." I shove more popcorn into my mouth to avoid speaking.

"Bullshit. There is so much to tell."

Instead of responding, I push the bowl back into her lap.

She continues, "I almost drowned in the pheromones and sexual tension when I got here."

"Trust me. Nothing is happening."

Her mouth pops open. "But something *has* happened?"

I am a terrible liar. My face burns.

She sits up straight, her mouth popping open. "I knew it!" She tosses a handful of popcorn at me.

"Hey!" I throw up a hand to thwart her, but I'm too late. Popcorn showers all over my lap and bounces onto the couch. I pick the food off my clothes and put it back in the bowl in her lap. "Nothing happened. It's nothing. And nothing is going to happen."

She picks up another handful and holds it up in a menacing gesture.

I point at her. "Don't throw that."

"I can't help myself. Curiosity makes me want to chuck things."

I raise my hands in surrender. "Okay, okay. Yes, he's attractive, but he's friends with the devil, and he's only here temporarily. I don't have feelings for him." I bite my lip and lower my hands. "But I might have pants feelings."

She grins and drops the popcorn back into the bowl. "Perfect. Release all your pants feelings on him while he's here."

I shake my head emphatically. "No. It's not happening."

"Why not? It doesn't have to be serious. It's not like you're gonna marry him. And he has a good aura."

I chuckle. "You aren't exactly the best judge of people."

Her mouth drops open. "I'm an excellent reader of people."

Exasperated, I give her the side-eye. "Taylor. You joined a cult."

"That was a phase, and I'm sorry, but Jared Leto is hot."

I laugh. "If you like the whole waif look, I guess."

"You clearly like them bigger." Her brows jog up and down.

Our laughter dies out, and we focus on the TV, lapsing into a comfortable silence.

Maybe Archer isn't the villain I thought he was, considering the past two days he's spent cleaning, fixing toilets, and doing a bunch of other terrible things, quickly and efficiently and without complaint. If I'm being honest with myself, it's been an immense relief.

Which is all the more reason I should avoid him. I don't want to like Archer, let alone admire him, but the more time I spend with him, the harder that becomes.

He's leaving eventually, and his end goal completely contradicts everything I've been working toward for years. We're at cross-purposes. I need to focus on my own objectives and stay away, avoid him at all costs.

Jacob snores and snuffles, and Taylor and I share an amused glance.

Maybe I can make Jake work with Archer during the day and answer some of his questions too. The idea sinks into my mind and settles. Yes. This could work. I can evade Archer and keep Jacob out of trouble at the same time. Maybe it will keep him occupied enough to push his drinking hours back, at least for a little bit.

CHAPTER
Eight

"What needs to get done next?"

"Well, let's see." Jacob scratches his jaw and then points at the truck parked in the drive. "The tires still have winter air in them. Can you take it to get switched out with some of that spring air?"

I resist the urge to release a beleaguered groan, but barely.

All morning, it's been like this. He sent me to get him a left-handed screwdriver and a back saw.

He asked me to check the size of his coveralls, and as soon as I was behind him, he ripped the biggest fart I've ever heard.

I've been indulging him through most of it, but my patience is fraying. There is actual work that could be done, and he's just making things harder for himself and Finley. "Listen, I get it. You want to mess with me because you think I'm the bad guy. But I swear to you, I'm not."

The lazy grin he's been throwing around all morning is gone when he stares me down and asks, "What are your intentions with my sister?"

I straighten to my full height. "Your sister is a grown woman who can handle herself."

"That's not really an answer." He glares at me.

"I promise you, I have no nefarious intentions against you or your sister. I respect her."

He frowns. "What? You don't respect me?"

I cross my arms over my chest. "I might respect you more if you stop sending me to get things like fallopian tubing or spirit level bubbles."

The grin returns, spreading his cheeks. "Come on, that was funny."

I shake my head. "You're wasting good help. Do you want to continue with the pranks, or do you want to actually accomplish something today?"

He stares at me for a few long seconds, considering. "Fine. You're right. But if you step out of line with my sister, this is a large property, and I know how to bury a body."

I nod, my stance relaxing. "I'm glad you're protective of her."

"Of course I am. She raised me. She's my sister, but she's also the only mother I've ever known."

Something tugs inside me at his words, but before I can examine my reaction too closely, he blows out a breath. "Come on. Let's go fix the trim and check the porch on cabin six. Last guest mentioned a loose screw in a board on one of the steps."

I follow him over to the garage to grab more supplies.

"I guess you're more than some hotshot from the city, huh?" He hands me a toolbox.

"My first job in high school was with a local contractor." I take it from him.

He picks up his own box of tools and looks me up and down. "No wonder Finley hasn't shot you yet."

An hour later, we're getting into a groove, working together pretty well, actually. He's not being a total ass except for the occasional ribbing, so we're managing to accomplish some things when Taylor shows up with sandwiches.

Before she relinquishes the food, she motions for us to keep working, and she takes some pictures of me, sweeping and dusting inside the cabin. She tries to get me to pose for a few of them, but I manage to dissuade her.

I don't mind helping Finley and the cottages, but the man-candy idea is distinctly unappealing.

We eat lunch in the sunshine on the front porch, Taylor keeping up a steady stream of conversation, talking about her travels, the last music festival she went to, and the upgrades she wants to make to her

VW bus. She's like a bright bubble of happiness, and I can't help but wonder at the contrast between her life and Finley's.

I haven't seen Finley since earlier this morning, when she told me I would be working with Jacob. She kept a complete stone face as she also told me that she couldn't answer any questions later, since Taylor will only be here a couple of days. She wants to spend some time with her family, but I am free to question Jacob about whatever I want while we work together.

After all that, she disappeared without a second glance.

Once we're done eating, Taylor pulls out her cell phone and shakes it at me.

"Archer, you have to get up on the ladder by that window. I want to get a shot of you using your hammer."

"Jesus, aren't you done ogling the man, Tay? We have actual work to finish here." Jacob stands up, wiping his hands on his jeans.

"Calm down, Jakey." She motions toward the window she wants me to pose by.

Jacob grumbles to himself and goes back to working on the porch steps, prying the nails off one of the boards.

I comply with her request, climbing up on the short ladder to reach the top of the window, where I had been renailing loose trim boards. I hold up the hammer and glance over at her. "Is this good?"

"Perfect. Now smile." She flashes me a wide grin and then snaps a few shots, reviewing them before giving me a thumbs-up to let me know she's finished.

I climb down and put the hammer back in the narrow toolbox on the patio.

"We have to run to the hardware store for lumber." Jacob stands up, nodding at me.

Taylor stomps down the sturdy side of the porch steps, patting Jacob on the shoulder as she passes. "You boys have fun. I'll upload these everywhere. Just wait. I bet this place will be fully booked by morning." She spins around, waving to us before bouncing back up to the main house.

I meet Jacob at the bottom of the porch, where he's frowning after her as she skips away.

He shakes his head with a sigh. "Right. We'll be fully booked, and she'll be gone." His gaze cuts back to mine. "You're driving."

"So hit me with some of these questions." Jacob waves a hand at me, leaning back in the passenger seat of the truck.

"What is your job around here?" Even though Finley already told me a little about Jacob's duties, I want him to go over everything he's responsible for in his own words.

"I run the website, do all the marketing, help the

customers, and whatever else she wants me to do."

"Did you go to school for any kind of marketing or business?"

He scoffs. "No. Barely made it through high school." He looks out the window at the blur of green pines flying by.

I attempt to dig a little deeper. "Is this what you want to do with your life? Do you plan on helping Finley run the business forever, or has there ever been anything else you wanted to do?"

His head turns toward me, scrutiny burning a hole in the side of my face. I keep my gaze trained on the road.

"There's nothing else I would want to do with my life. Nowhere else I would want to go. Whitby is my home."

I take a second to glance over at him and nod. "Understood."

"Is that your game here? Trying to act like you're understanding, but really, you're trying to find a way to get us to give up our home so your buddy can buy it?"

"No," I say, but then I hesitate and add gently, "Not really."

He gives me a side eye along with a disbelieving chuckle.

"At least I'm honest."

"I guess. Any other probing questions?"

I pull into the parking lot at the hardware store and

find a spot in the front. "What's your GOPPAR?"

I put the car in park and look over at him.

He squints at me. "I don't see how it's any of your business if I have an STD, but the answer is I don't. I'm totally clean."

I stifle a smile. "It means gross operating profit per available room."

"Oh." He shrugs. "Not something I'm aware of. You'll have to ask Finley, but I doubt she knows either. She never went to college for any marketing or business or anything either. We do the best we can with what we have."

We get out of the car, and I follow him into the barnlike structure.

"Hey, Bonnie," Jacob calls out to the elderly woman behind the counter.

"Well, hey there, Jacob. What brings you in today— oh. Who's your friend?"

Bonnie is eighty if she's a day. Her eyes move up and down behind her thick, plastic-framed glasses. Her hair is dyed a pale pink, and she's wearing bright-red lipstick.

"This is Archer." Jacob leans his elbows on the counter. "He's helping us out for a few days."

"Weeks," I say.

"Maybe one week."

"Maybe two," I counter.

Her gaze volleys back and forth between us before landing on me with something beyond a grandmotherly smile. "So nice to have a new face in town, and such a handsome one at that." She moves around the counter and approaches me with her hand extended. She shakes my hand for a few seconds, and instead of letting go, she continues to clutch my palm in one hand while patting the top with her other.

"Mom, stop harassing the customers." A middle-aged man emerges from the back.

"Oh, hush, Elliot." She turns back to me. "That's my son. He's such a buzzkill." Her tone is sweet as can be, a smile plastered to her lips.

"Hey, Jake." Elliot ignores his mother. "Can I help you?"

"I need to get some six-inch deck boards."

"Only six inches?" Bonnie turns away, releasing my hand.

"Ma," Elliot groans.

I move away, escaping while I can under the pretense of searching for something down the aisles, perusing their inventory in case there's anything else I need to get for the cabins while I'm here.

It's a fairly well-stocked hardware store. They have paint, nuts and bolts, car maintenance items, plumbing, housewares, office supplies . . . My gaze snags on a desk set covered in daisies.

Flower-edged Post-it notes and a notepad, binder clips with daisies painted on them, a business card holder, pens, and a penholder. I snag it before I think too much about it and head back up to the front desk.

Bonnie has disappeared somewhere along with Elliot, and a young woman is ringing Jacob up for the deck boards. Pink floods her face as she fiddles with the register.

Jacob's back is to me, his hands shoved into his pockets, the line of his shoulders tense.

I stop next to him and put the desk set on the counter. "This, too, please." I pull out my wallet to pay for the lot.

"I thought you moved away," Jacob says to the woman behind the counter.

She's pretty. Dark hair, heart-shaped face, probably around Jacob's age.

"I'm in town visiting for a couple days." She smiles weakly and pushes more buttons on the register. It bleats, a harsh, discordant noise.

She winces and then takes a breath, her gaze flickering over me for a second before returning to Jacob.

"I'm glad we ran into each other though." She swallows, and her throat bobs with the movement. "I've been wanting to talk to you about . . . well, everything." She uses a hand to brush a loose strand of hair behind her ear. "Do you want to go get a drink or some coffee or something? I'm leaving town soon, but I'm free tonight. We could go get ribs at Veronica's? I know it's your favorite." She grabs the desk set from in front of me and scans it.

Jacob rubs the back of his neck with one hand. "I can't. I have—" He looks over at me, and his face clears. "My friend here. Archer." He slaps me on the back with more force than I expect, making me jump. "He, uh… We're really busy today."

Poor woman. Her mouth goes tight.

I smile at her and then glance over at Jacob. "It's fine if you want to—"

"No, no, no. It's not fine. We have things. Remember." His eyes lock with mine. Beseeching.

"Oh." I turn to face the counter. "Yes. Right. That really important appointment we have today."

Jacob nods emphatically. "Yes. An appointment." He grabs the word like a lifeline.

A thought strikes me. A little friendly payback. "It's a doctor's appointment," I explain to her, handing over my credit card. "Itching for a long time down there isn't normal. We need to get this guy checked out right away." I clap him on the back, harder than he hit me.

He stumbles against the counter. Instead of getting offended or giving me a dark glare, once he gets his footing, Jacob plays right along. "Right." He nods solemnly. "I have GOPPAR."

Surprised laughter bursts out of me, and I turn it into a cough.

"What is that?" A crease between her brows, concern making her lips tip down.

"That's what we hope to find out," Jacob says, his voice grave.

"I hope it isn't serious." She hands me back my card

and the receipt, and I grab the bag with the desk set while Jacob picks up the wood.

"It's fine. Thanks, see you around."

He hustles me out the door, and when we're in the car, I turn to him with a questioning glance. "What was that all about?"

Jacob shakes his head. "Nothing. It's nothing. Thanks for your help back there, man." He chuckles. "Itching. That was pretty good."

"Hey. I need help with cabin five." The screen door slams behind Finley as she exits the front office the next morning.

I stand up from where I've been waiting for her on the front steps of the main house.

"We have a family of four coming in a couple of hours, and that's the only decent cabin left with two beds. I cleaned it a few weeks ago, and no one's been in there since, so we just need to make sure everything works and dust things off. The last guests mentioned the heater was acting up, but I haven't had time to check it out, so I might need help with it."

"Okay." I follow her down the gravel road to the cabin in silence.

Once we reach it, Finley unlocks the door, and we tread inside.

"Do you smell that?" She wrinkles her nose at me.

"Maybe someone left some garbage behind that you missed before?"

"I guess." She leaves the door open to air it out and moves further into the room, rubbing her arms. "It's freezing in here."

She keeps the radiators set low in all the vacant cabins—high enough to keep the pipes from freezing but low enough to save on energy costs.

She walks over to the radiator and turns the knob, fiddling with it for a minute. "This doesn't seem to be working." A line forms between her brows, the corner of her lips tugging downward.

"I'll check the breaker." I jog outside to make sure a circuit hasn't blown. Then I head back in to find her already taking it apart to reach the diverter valve and flicking it on and off.

"Nope. This isn't working." She blows out an exasperated exhale.

"I can try cleaning the pump."

Our gazes lock. She presses her lips together and then nods.

"That would be great. I'll work on prepping the rest of the place and trying to figure out where the stench is coming from." She winces. "If this doesn't work, though, I have nowhere else to place them—nowhere with enough beds."

I crouch down to check out the radiator more closely. "We'll figure it out."

She doesn't move right away, and after a few

seconds I look up.

She's staring down at me, her expression inscrutable. "Thank you."

"You're welcome."

She still doesn't move right away. "Thank you for the office supplies too. I love daisies."

"I noticed."

The corner of her mouth lifts, and then she turns away.

It was almost a smile. Progress.

I get to work taking out the pump and checking for leaks inside the heater, making sure none of the vents are blocked, while she moves around the rest of the space, dusting, sweeping, checking that the bathroom is stocked with mini shampoo and whatnot.

I try to focus on the task at hand and not her presence fluttering around the room behind me, but it's like I'm eternally aware of her movements, her breathing patterns, every little sound she makes.

Which is why when she starts clearing out the closet—this one has a slightly larger walk-in area with a dresser pushed to the back—I'm immediately tuned in to her sudden stillness.

I stand up, already stepping toward the closet where she disappeared, when there's a strange chittering sound then growling.

Finley screams, the sound piercing and terrified.

She races out of the closet, still shrieking, and heads straight for me.

Nine

FINLEY

I sprint toward Archer and collide with him in the center of the room.

My heart is thundering in my ears, my entire body is shaking. I grip his shoulders, trying to climb him in my panic.

"What is it?" His arms wrap around me, solid and secure and grounding. His voice is a calm rumble, and I couldn't let go of him right now even if my life depended on it.

"There's something in there." I raise one trembling hand toward the closet.

"A mouse or something?"

"No." I shake my head. "It was bigger than that. A lot bigger." I shudder, and his arms tighten around me.

"What did it look like?"

"I don't know. I didn't have the light on, so it was a little hard to see. It was big. Like a rabid dog or something. Should we call animal control?"

He moves away from me to check it out.

I grip his shirt. "Wait, no. We should leave."

"Let me take a look. Just stay over here."

I stand behind him, not releasing my grip on his clothes. I stare down at his ass. Damn, that's nice. It actually calms me down, ogling Archer's butt. It's a magic ass.

He peeks carefully into the closet. "I don't see anything."

"Something was in there. I swear it."

His head tilts down at the ground. "There's a bunch of trash in here."

"Yes! I was picking it up and heading toward the dresser—there seems to be more over there—and that's when I saw it, and it attacked me." I shudder again.

He glances at me over his shoulder. "Attacked you?"

"Okay, fine, it stared at me, made some godawful noise, and then disappeared behind the dresser when I started screaming."

"Is there a light switch?"

I point past his head. "There's a chain you can pull over there."

He steps into the closet, and I remain on the

outside, not brave enough to enter the space, even accompanied by the magic ass.

He tugs on the cord, and the space lights up.

Wrappers and bits of plastic are strewn all over the floor, along with something that might be flour or sugar. There are tracks in it.

Archer crouches and points to one perfect little handprint.

"Raccoon."

I groan. "Those thieving little bastards."

He chuckles, standing, and I smack him on the arm. "It's not funny. I should have guessed. They were romping through the trash up at the house the other night. How did they get in here?"

"They can fit in surprisingly small spaces. We'll have to check outside for where he got in."

I cover my face with a hand. It's always something.

He stands and walks toward me, rubbing the outsides of my arms with warm palms. "It will be fine."

I shouldn't do it. But it's like I'm not even in control of my body. I lean into him.

His arms open immediately, cocooning me in warmth.

I rest my head against his chest, listening to the steady thud of his heartbeat and relishing the heat of him.

It's wrong to be using him like this, for affection and consolation, when I've been avoiding him and being a total jerk. Is he only putting up with me because of Oliver and what he wants?

I step back out of the circle of his embrace and immediately feel chilled. "Sorry."

His arms drop to his sides. "It's not a problem."

I wrap my arms around myself.

"We should check outside." He heads out the front door without waiting.

I take a deep breath and follow.

I find him around back. He's leaning over near the foundation, and he stands as I approach. "There's an entry point here." He gestures down at a spot low in the siding that's gone soft and has broken apart. "I think you scared him away for now. I'll close this off with some plywood from the shed. But it stinks pretty bad in there. Our little buddy may have been using the space between the walls as a toilet."

I groan and cover my face with my hands. "What do I tell the guests? There's not enough time to fix this, clean, and air it out before they get here."

"What about giving them two cabins?"

She shakes her head. "They want one cabin with two beds because they have little kids. I'd hate to cancel; they booked a month ago. We can't afford bad business."

He rubs his chin, considering. "They can have my cabin. I have two beds, and everything works fine. It will be easy enough to change the sheets and clean it out."

"Then where will you sleep?"

Our eyes lock.

"I can stay somewhere in town for the night."

"Stay up at the house." The words pop out of my mouth without passing through my brain. "We have plenty of rooms."

He examines my face for a few long seconds, and then one corner of his mouth tips up. "Okay."

I've upgraded from dirty jeans and boots to clean jeans and ballet flats.

"What are you doing?" Jacob leans in the doorway, brows furrowed, arms crossed over his chest.

Since I basically live in work clothes and pajamas, getting dressed up in anything other than dirty jeans or sweats is akin to wearing a ball gown.

I lean back from the mirror over my dresser and shove the mascara wand back into the container. "Nothing."

"Are you going out? I thought I smelled food."

"I'm not going out. And yes, there's food. I'm making roast chicken." I frown at him in the mirror. "Are you going to be home for dinner?" Taylor left, so I thought he'd be neck deep in a bottle of something or other. He's not slurring his speech, but his eyes are a bit glassy, his skin tinged with pink. Ugh. One of those nights where he's been drinking just enough to pretend at sobriety. We'll see how long it lasts.

He frowns. "Why wouldn't—?"

A knock downstairs cuts him off.

His scowl deepens. "Are you expecting someone?"

I bustle past him. "Just Archer. We needed his cabin for the guests that came earlier today. So he's staying here tonight."

He chuckles and trails behind me. "Is that why you're getting all dressed up? Did you . . . did you cook for him?"

"I cooked for all of us."

We pound down the stairs. "Do you like this guy? I thought Taylor was messing with you, but she was right. You like him." He makes kissy noises.

I stop in the living room and turn to face him. "What are you, a child?"

He rubs the back of his head, a sheepish expression on his face. "Sorta."

I resist the urge to check my hair one more time in the mirror above the fireplace. "Will you clean your tools off the dining table?"

Jacob makes a face. "Are you trying to impress him or something?"

"No, I just want to have somewhere to sit that isn't the couch. Is that too much to ask? That we eat like a normal family?"

"It's the normal part that's weird." But he starts picking up his stuff despite the grumbling.

I head to the side door, where Archer's frame is visible through the beveled glass. My stomach flutters, and I take a few breaths to calm my racing heart. I saw him a couple hours ago. Why am I nervous?

I open the door.

Archer stands on the stoop, holding a duffle bag, still wearing the jeans and sweater from earlier.

"Hey. Can I use your shower? Sorry, but I didn't want the one in my cabin to be recently used when the other guests arrived."

I step back to let him in. "Oh, of course. I'll show you the room and where everything is."

The flutters in my stomach morph into vigorous flaps of activity.

Calm down. It's no big deal.

I point out the bathroom and where the towels are stored then take him to his room at the end of the hall. He's staying in Mindy and Taylor's old bedroom. The house has five bedrooms upstairs: the master; Mindy and Taylor's old room; Piper's bedroom, which I moved into when I moved back home; Jacob's room; and my childhood bedroom, which Aria had taken over when I moved out. We tend to avoid Dad's and Aria's old spaces.

"Are you hungry?" I hover in the doorway.

He looks over my outfit with a confused smile. "Are you offering to poison me?" He tosses his duffle bag onto the bed and then bends over to unlace his shoes.

It's more intimate than I would have thought, watching him take off his shoes.

I try not to smile. "Jacob's eating too. He can be your tester."

He grabs some clothes from his bag and stops next to me in the doorway. "Sounds like you could kill two big birds with one poisonous stone." He smiles at me, and it's as potent as an electric jolt.

We're standing too close. He smells kind of like dirt and kind of like cleaning supplies, but for some reason, I don't mind it.

"I'll be eating too."

His eyes rove over my face. "I'm starving, actually, and it smells amazing."

I think he's referring to the food, but my brain scrambles anyway.

My gaze dips to his mouth. After a second, he slides away.

The bathroom door shuts softly, and then the water kicks on.

I'm still in the doorway, staring at nothing.

I do not want to think about him naked in my shower.

ARCHER

When I emerge, clean and refreshed, I find Finley in the kitchen chopping tomatoes for a salad.

I pause before entering, stopping to take a second and view her unobserved. Her hair is down, long and wavy. She's wearing skinny jeans, dark ballet flats, and a T-shirt that hugs her curves to perfection.

I'm tempted to stare at her longer, but there's a fine line between admiration and creep. Besides, I can't act on these feelings, even though something has definitely shifted between us. She's been less guarded since the raccoon incident.

"Do you need help with anything?"

She spins to face me, her gaze dipping for a second to take in my attire—nothing fancy: a long-sleeved black Henley with gray sweatpants. She bites her bottom lip and then gives me her back.

"Will you set the table?" she says over her shoulder, gesturing with her knife to the plates sitting on the counter. "I don't know where Jacob ran off to."

I grab the dishes, stopping next to her for a second. "Why are you feeding me?"

She scoops up some chopped tomato using the flat edge of the knife and drops it into the bowl. "The past few days have been terrible. I made sure of it. But despite all evidence to the contrary, I'm not a total dick."

"I didn't think you were."

She puts the knife down and faces me, resting a hip against the counter. "Plus, you saved my ass from the killer raccoon."

"They are rather nefarious."

One side of her mouth curves. "I'm sure I saw him twirling his handlebar moustache."

"Those raccoons sure know how to maintain their facial hair."

Just when I think I'm going to get a genuine smile, the side door bangs open.

"Where were you?" Finley asks Jacob.

"Putting away my tools from the table like you asked."

She watches him for a second and then nods. "Dinner's about ready. Will you bring the chicken and rolls to the table?"

I follow him into the dining room with the plates, and Finley joins us with the salad and forks.

We arrange ourselves at one end of the giant oak table, which is large enough to seat a family of eight. Jacob takes the place at the head, and Finley and I sit across from each other.

After a few minutes spent dishing out food and passing items around, a stilted silence descends.

"So, Archer." Jacob stabs some lettuce with his fork. "Did you have a happy childhood, or are you funny?"

"Jacob!" Finley's tone is exasperated.

"Never mind," he continues. "I already know you aren't that funny."

I finish chewing a bite of chicken. "Weird. You laughed when I pretended you had an STD."

He chuckles and points his fork at me. "That was kind of funny."

"STD?" Finley glances back and forth between the two of us.

"Willow's in town," Jacob explains. "She wanted to hang out. Archer saved me from a potentially disastrous situation."

"Willow? How is she?"

"Fine, I guess." He shoves a bite of salad into his mouth.

"Why didn't you want to hang out with her?"

He stops, his fork halfway to his mouth, and gives her an incredulous look. "You really have to ask?"

"I guess not." She watches him for a few seconds

before she picks up her water and takes a sip.

I really want to know, but there are undercurrents here that I can't quite read, and I don't want to interfere.

"Oh, before I forget." He scratches his chin. "I need the truck tomorrow."

"You can't take it tomorrow. Tomorrow's Saturday. I have class."

"I already promised Frank I'd give him a ride to see his grandma tomorrow morning. She's in a nursing home. I couldn't say no."

"We need the money, Jacob."

"I can drop you off early before I work around here and then pick you up a little late."

A muscle in her jaw twitches.

"I can drive you," I interject, slicing into the tension building between them.

"That's great. Thanks, man," Jacob says, tossing me a smile.

Finley glares at him then points the sharp gaze at me before staring down at her plate.

I open my mouth to say something, apologize, ask what is going on, I don't even know, but before I can say anything further, Jacob speaks.

"See? Problem solved. Besides, you'll need me to be close to town in case any of our guests have issues, since we're booked up this weekend."

Finley grinds out, "Fine." Then she picks up a roll and takes a big bite.

Jacob finishes his plate and then stands. "I'm going out. Be home later." He takes his plate into the kitchen, and a few seconds later, the side door opens and shuts.

She sits back in her seat and looks at me. "I'm sorry about that."

"There's nothing for you to be sorry for. I'm sorry I intervened."

She winces. "No. It's fine. I wasn't upset that you offered to drive me. I appreciate the offer. It's just that . . . I don't like Frank. He's not a good influence on Jacob." She rubs the side of her head. "Maybe they aren't a good influence on each other. Anyway, I was hoping if he *had* to drive me, he wouldn't be spending the day drinking with Frank."

She leans forward and spears a piece of chicken with her fork but doesn't eat it, just stares down at it.

"Ah. Well if you want, I could make up some excuse."

She considers and then shakes her head. "No. We'll fight, he'll drop me off early and pick me up late, if he remembers at all, then use it as an excuse to go on a bender for the rest of the weekend." She sticks the chicken into her mouth and chews for a second.

"How long have you been dealing with this?" I'm not sure if she'll answer, but I'm curious enough to risk it.

"Actually, he didn't drink much until Dad died, but since then, it's gotten progressively worse."

"I'm sorry."

"So am I." She sets her fork down and stares at it. "The problems really started when he was fifteen."

"Fifteen?"

"That's when Aria died. They were twins." Her gaze shutters.

I conjure the image of the photos lining the halls upstairs. I knew she had a big family, I knew her parents were gone, but I didn't realize she had lost a sibling. And so young.

Before I can offer any kind of trite condolences, she continues, her gaze focused on her plate.

"Willow was Aria's best friend," she explains.

"I was wondering about that. She seems like a nice person. I couldn't figure out why he was avoiding her."

"He's avoiding her because he avoids any kind of conversation that might relate to anything about Aria. He never speaks about her at all. I don't think I've heard him so much as speak her name in the past ten years."

"It must cause him a lot of pain."

"Oh, yeah." She slumps back in her seat. "He almost didn't graduate from high school. If it wasn't for Dad and me pushing him all the time, he probably would have dropped out. Then he wanted to join the military at eighteen, but we worried it was because he had a death wish. He stayed because Dad got sick, and he helped to take care of him, which kept him focused on something else. And now . . ."

"Now he's using alcohol as an escape."

She picks up her napkin and rubs the corner between her fingers. "I wish I could, too, sometimes."

"Problems don't go away when we avoid them."

"Don't I know it. I'm sorry. I didn't mean to unload that on you. Aren't you glad you came over for dinner?" She releases a short laugh. "I better clean up." She stands, picking up her plate.

I follow her lead, getting up and gathering the remaining dishes.

We carry everything into the kitchen. She stores the leftover food in the fridge, and I start on washing the dirty dishes.

"I can finish up." She stops next to me at the sink.

"You cooked; I can clean. Fair's fair. If you want to go relax, go. I can handle a few dishes."

"Thank you. I'm pretty wiped. I'll see you in the morning?"

"Sounds good. What time do you need to leave?"

"Nine thirty or so."

I nod, and she disappears.

My thoughts are a buzz in my head. Their family life is more complicated than I first realized. What would it be like to lose a sibling, a twin at that? And at such a young age? Finley would have been fairly young too. If Jacob was fifteen, she would have been, what? Twenty-one? Twenty-two at most? Just starting adulthood, and then to be delivered such a blow.

It's clear she's doing everything she can to take care

of this place for her family. For Jacob. Perhaps part of the reason they're so attached to the land is because it's where Aria lived and died. I have no doubts that Finley would do anything for her family. She's not the type of person to run or avoid, no matter how hard things get.

Jacob doesn't realize how lucky he is.

After the dishes are done and drying in the rack, I wipe off the counters and the dining table. The house is quiet. It's still fairly early, but I don't want to stay downstairs alone.

I head up to my room and try to call Nora. She doesn't answer. I pull out my laptop, but the Wi-Fi isn't the greatest, and it takes fifteen minutes for my email box to load three messages. I grab a book from the shelf in the bedroom I'm in, but it's an old V.C. Andrews novel, and I'm creeped out by page three.

I'll go downstairs to get some water or something. That will kill a few minutes.

In the long hallway, I pause by the wall of photos, perusing them with fresh eyes.

My gaze snags on a picture of Finley posing on an ice rink in a sparkly leotard. She looks to be fourteen or thereabouts, her hair braided like a crown around her head, a wide smile stretching her lips.

Taylor's familiar face pops out at me. I stop on one photo where she's laughing and hugging one of their sisters in front of a school—maybe a middle school based on their youthful smiling faces. The other sister is younger and could be a female version of Jacob.

Aria.

Is it her?

I scan the photos, searching for more of the little sister.

There. One of her and Jacob dressed up as Harry Potter and Hermione Granger. They can't be more than ten years old, holding up their wands to the camera.

I scrub a hand through my hair. No wonder Jacob is messed up.

A door creaks open, and Finley steps into the hallway, blinking at the overhead light.

"Hi. Sorry. Did I wake you?"

"No. I was just reading." She pads over to me, wearing only an oversized T-shirt, giving me more than a decent glimpse of her slender legs.

My whole body tightens, including certain parts of my anatomy that still have fond memories of what it's like to be pressed tight against the heat between her legs.

Is she trying to kill me?

"Didn't you already see all of this the other night?"

"I didn't get a good look. There are so many of them."

I point out a picture of all five sisters lined up together, arms around each other, some smiling, some making faces.

"This is you." I tap on Finley, standing on the far end. "And Taylor." Taylor is second from the end on the other side. The youngest sister, who must be Aria, is standing next to her and giving her bunny ears.

"Who's this one?" I point out the dark-haired teen next to Finley, who looks to be of an age with Finley in the photo.

"Mindy. She's a year younger than me. Then Piper."

"The artist?"

She nods.

Piper is smack dab in the middle.

"Then Taylor, then Aria."

I review more photos, one of Piper standing in front of a giant metal sculpture of a man on a bicycle.

"Did she do this piece?" I point to it.

"Yes."

My brows shoot up. "Wow. That's all metalwork?"

"Yes." Her face glows with pride. "She does commissioned and original work using metal and copper and bronze and the like. Dad got her into welding when she was a girl, around eight."

"A strange hobby for a grade schooler."

She chuckles. "Right? But she had a knack for it. He showed her how to do it when he was making barbecue pits, and that was all it took for her to get hooked. She practiced all the time, making whatever she could out of materials she found in trash cans, at school, anywhere, really. Then she was discovered in high school. A guest from the city who stayed here one summer was an art collector."

"That's amazing."

"It really is."

I glance over some other group photos, including Jacob and their father.

I squint at one of Mindy. "Is this Mindy with . . . Paul McCartney?"

She nods. "She works for a music label in New York. Rebel Records."

"Wow."

"Yeah. I'm really proud of her." Her tone is wistful. "I'm proud of all of them."

Even Jacob? I wonder, but I don't push it. It's clear losing his twin crushed his entire world, and the pieces never reassembled, which is understandable, if tragic.

"What does she do at the record label?"

"She's a manager. I'm not sure exactly what it entails, but I know she's busy all the time."

"That sounds like an interesting job. Successful too. And your sister Piper is a well-known artist." I shove my hands into my pockets and look over at Finley. "Why don't your sisters help you?"

She flinches, a slight movement I might not have noticed if I hadn't been watching her closely.

I wince. "Sorry. You don't have to answer."

She hesitates. "No. It's fine. They have helped me in the past, but I can't keep asking them. Everyone relinquished all rights over the property to me after Dad died. No one else wanted to deal with it, but it's our home. This is for me to deal with."

"Because you're the oldest?"

"Because I have to." Her chin lifts.

I have to admire her tenacity. "You're doing the best you can with what you have."

She snorts out a laugh that's halfway to a sob. "Is that condescension?"

"No. Anyone else would have given up by now."

"Would you?"

I shove my hands into my pockets again. "No. I wouldn't. I understand why you can't let it go."

"Then why are you still here?"

"I want to come up with a plan that will please everyone. That's my job—it's my mission in business, in life . . . to make people happy."

She turns toward me, arms crossed over her chest. "Who makes you happy?"

The question is like a direct strike to the chest.

I don't know what makes me answer. Maybe it's how candid and open Finley has been tonight. Maybe it's because we're standing in the narrow space of the hallway, under the watchful eyes of her family history.

I take a breath and then meet her eyes, her inquisitive gaze that was once challenging and is now thoughtful.

The words fall out, stark and succinct and brutally honest. "No one."

I walk past her and into my room, shutting the door on her bewildered expression.

FINLEY

"Why are you calling me so early on a Saturday?" Mindy's voice is bleary with sleep.

"It's nine o'clock." I never get to sleep in past seven.

She groans. "I didn't get home till two this morning."

I lean back in the office chair, my foot bouncing. "You didn't have to answer the phone."

She yawns. "You know I always will when it's you."

"I do. And I appreciate it."

Blankets rustle in the background. "What's going on?"

I page through some mail on the desk. Bills, that's

what's going on. Second notices, final invoices, pay-now-or-we'll-make-you-fish-meal type of letters.

Wincing, I shove them to the side and lean forward to click on an incoming email. "Not too much. Just working and giving you a call to see what you're doing for Easter."

I'm making an attempt at multitasking while I talk to Mindy on speakerphone.

"Easter?" Her tired voice turns incredulous. "Come on, Fin, what's this really about?"

"I'm serious. I want to try to get all of us together, maybe even Piper."

"But *Easter*?" She laughs. "We don't go to church, and we're too old to decorate eggs or have an egg hunt or anything like that."

"We're never too old to be a family together. It will be fun." I inject enthusiasm into my voice as if it will help even though I know it's more likely the chair I'm sitting in will sprout arms and do cartwheels around the room. We haven't all been in the same room in more than a year.

"I'll put it on my calendar." She chuckles. "But I doubt this dream will be realized. It would require prying Piper from the paws of that . . . *Ben*." His name is a curse word. "Not to mention getting Taylor to leave whatever hippie-dippie bullshit she's meandered her way into."

Her voice cuts out when another call beeps on the line.

It's Reed. Again. Ugh. *I still can't pay the tax bill.* I'm glad we aren't dating anymore. It would just make everything that much more awkward.

I send him to voicemail, where he can linger along with all the other debtors calling and looking for their due. I keep talking. "Taylor saw Piper last month. She said she seemed okay."

"Like Taylor could tell? Seriously. Ben looks like someone you'd see on the ID channel."

"I'm not sure what we can do about it."

"I know." She releases a weak sigh. "She's a grown woman. The last time we talked, I told her point-blank she should leave him. Now she won't respond to my calls or texts."

"Same here. When I bring him up at all, it makes her withdraw more, which doesn't accomplish anything."

"You can't help someone if they don't think they need it."

A soft knock taps at the door, and Archer appears. "Hey. You ready? I've got the car warming up. Is this your bag?" He nods to my large duffle.

It's stuffed full of my ice skates, snacks, and extra laces and other necessities.

Before I can respond, Mindy speaks. "Um, excuse me, who is that with the sultry voice?"

"It's no one." I make throat-slashing motions at Archer.

He smiles.

"Doesn't sound like no one."

"I'm Archer," he calls out.

Mindy gasps in delight. "Who is Archer? Archer, who are you?"

"I'll call you later, Mindy. I'm hanging up now."

"He sounds hot. You have something else you want to share, Fin?" She gets out right before I hit the end call button.

My face is on fire.

I shove my cell into the side pocket of my leggings. "I'm ready." We're going to pretend none of that just happened.

Archer is grinning at me, lifting my bag off the floor. "Do you need help with anything else before we go?"

My shoulders slump, relieved he's not going to mention Mindy's parting comments.

"No. We should be good."

We walk out to his car, and he puts my bag in the back seat before opening the passenger door for me.

Within minutes, we're on the road, tires humming over the pavement. I focus out the window so I don't stare at his rugged profile.

We sit in comfortable silence for the first few miles.

"How long have you been teaching ice skating?" he asks as he's getting on the interstate toward Binghampton.

"A few years now."

"Do you enjoy it?"

"I love it. I wish I could do it more. There's nothing better than seeing a kid land a jump for the first time. My morning classes are groups of younger kids, and in the afternoon, I offer private lessons."

"Are any of them good?" he asks.

I smile, thinking about how Trina placed in the National Showcase last month. "Yes. A few of them are at competition level."

"You must be a good teacher."

I wave off the compliment. "I try. Thanks again for taking me. You sure you're going to have enough to keep you busy for six hours?"

"I'll be fine. I have work to do since I've been otherwise occupied the past few days." He gives me a sidelong look. "Do you like teaching better than managing the cottages?"

I snort out a laugh. "I don't *like* running the cottages."

My breath stutters to a stop in my throat. The words hang there in the air between us like one of those conversation bubbles in a comic strip.

I didn't even realize the thought existed in my head until I said it out loud. Where did those words come from?

Is it true? It can't be. My family property is everything to me. I love my home.

But the business . . . my heart has never been in the manual labor and transactional duties involved.

I never went to college. I barely went to high

school, attending just enough to graduate, since most of my time was spent training and competing.

Dad paid a lot of money for choreographers and coaches, something I didn't quite realize until I took over the business and got a look at the finances.

On top of that, Jacob will never leave, not for anything, and he needs me.

But what if I'm making excuses? What if I can't give it up because I've been focused on it for so long that I can't even remember what it's like to make decisions for myself?

What if throwing myself into saving the cabins is my own form of escape? Something I can control, since I can't control so many things. It's not much of an escape though; it's more of a duty. It's like if I keep our home alive, then I'm keeping Aria alive too. At least her memory. And maybe our family will come together again, someday, if only we still have our home.

Archer has been quiet for a few minutes, letting me fester in my thoughts.

But now he asks gently, "Do you even want to do it anymore?"

I grip the armrest. "It doesn't matter what I want."

"Of course it matters. It matters most."

I stare out the window at the passing scenery, not wanting to examine my own thoughts. Not now, not ever. I tilt my head to observe Archer as he passes a semi-truck.

All the questions that were tumbling through my

head last night, after he left me in the hallway when he made his pronouncement, reappear. *No one*, he said. I haven't been able to stop thinking about it. I shouldn't want to know anything about him. I don't want to find him so intriguing, and I shouldn't care. But I can't help it.

"How did you meet Oliver?"

He tosses me a quick glance before answering. "We met when we were kids."

"School?"

"Summer camp."

I take that piece of information and slide it into place with the rest of the puzzle that is Archer Weston, and something clicks. "Wait. You met at a summer camp, and he wants to turn Fox Cottages into a camp for disadvantaged kids . . . Is that how you met?"

He nods. "Yes. At Camp Velveteen in New Hampshire. We were bunkmates, and he hated me at first." His smile is wry. "He even tried to fight me a couple of times."

My brows lift. "Really?"

He chuckles. "He was a scrawny little thing, and I've never been small. It wasn't much of a fight. I didn't hurt him too much though."

"How did you become friends then?"

He doesn't answer for a few long seconds.

"Sorry. Too personal." I wince. "You don't have to tell me."

"It's not that." His hand shifts on the steering

wheel. "Well, it's partly that. Some of it is more personal for Oliver than me, and it's kind of a long story."

"Short version?"

He considers his answer before speaking. "We had to band together against some rougher boys."

"The enemy of my enemy is my friend?"

"Something like that."

Curiosity prods me. I want to know more, more about why he was there—what was Archer's childhood like? What about his family, his parents?

But I can't ask. It's not fair, is it? It's too personal. We've gotten too close for comfort already, shared too much. I'm finding that he's impossible to not like.

If he opens his mouth and tells me he overcame significant adversity to become this generous and hardworking person I'm coming to know, the attraction would be inescapable. I wouldn't be able to stay away, to keep him at arm's length.

"He wants to create a camp because of his childhood. Because it was a happy place for him?"

"Something like that."

"But why *my* land? He's rich enough. He could probably buy a whole damn island somewhere."

One big shoulder shifts up and down. "It's the location relative to where he lives, the size, the creek and pond, and probably other things. Oliver is like a dog with a bone. He gets an idea about something, and you can't make him shake it. His intentions are admirable. His methods, perhaps not so much."

As altruistic as it all sounds, I'm still not selling.

We enter the city limits of Binghampton, and I direct Archer down some side streets and toward the rink. It's a large, circular concrete stadium that hosts local hockey games in addition to practices and various ice-skating classes and events.

I point to the cluster of parents and kids crowded around the main entrance. "You can pull up by that group of people. They must have the doors locked still."

He parks, and before I can warn him, he jumps out to grab my bag for me.

I manage to get out of the car before he can open the door for me, but I'm too late to stop the inevitable.

"Finley, is this one of your brothers?" Carol Anne, a single mom who has two girls in my class, has already sidled up to introduce herself, shaking his free hand even as he sets the bag on the ground at my feet.

"I only have one brother, and you've met him."

"Oh, right. The young one." Her nose wrinkles then smooths out when she looks up at Archer and smiles.

"Well, this one is much more mature," Greg cuts in, shooting a glance to his partner, James.

"Finley, Finley! I lost a tooth!" One of the kids, Samuel, runs up, tugging on my sleeve.

Rebecca comes up behind him. "One time, the tooth

fairy didn't take my tooth for three days. Mommy said sometimes she gets tired."

Samuel and Rebecca start arguing over whether the tooth fairy sleeps, and I give Archer an apologetic grimace.

It's pure chaos, and I just got here.

Archer takes it in stride, smiling and nodding at everyone crowding around. "I'll be back in a couple hours," he says to me. Then, like the smart man he is, he makes his escape. "Text me if you need anything," he calls out before climbing back into the car.

"He is a tall drink of water, and honey, I am thirsty," Carol Anne tells me.

James nudges Greg. "That one doesn't have to put the cookies in the oven. He just walks by and winks at it."

They all laugh, and I press my lips together.

Carol Anne nudges me with her elbow. "You gonna share?"

"He's not my boyfriend."

"Thank the heavens. Can I have him?"

"No." He drives away, and then I turn to face her. "You can't."

CHAPTER
Twelve

Archer

I stop at a coffee shop next to the Chenango River and set up at a table inside with my laptop and a notepad and pen.

My email box is slammed with a ton of stuff from Nora, current clients, past clients, my accountant, and upcoming appointments. It takes me an hour to wade through it all and organize them by priority.

There's one from Oliver with no subject line that says, "call me."

At least he hasn't been blowing up my phone, and I didn't tell him he couldn't email me, so I'm not surprised he immediately found a way to get around my "don't call me" rule.

Knowing I can't put off the inevitable forever, I call him.

He answers on the first ring. "Tell me good news."

"I'm coming up with some ideas." Sort of.

The fact that Finley admitted she doesn't enjoy running the cabins gives me hope that there is a resolution—one in which she can keep the memory of her sister alive and keep her family home but also find a way for her to chase her own happiness. Now I need to figure out how to work that into Oliver's endgame. I don't know when her desires became tantamount to my own goals, but here we are.

It has to be the physical attraction, the ever-present burn of want, and now it's been combined with respect for all she's done, her innate strength, and how she takes care of her family. It's not often I feel a connection to anyone. And by not often, I mean never.

"I don't want ideas, Archer. I want a sale."

"Is that the end goal? I thought you wanted a camp."

"It's the same thing."

I tap my pen against the tabletop. "What if I can get you the result you want but without the sale?"

"What's the point if I don't own it?"

I understand his need to be in charge, but I don't like it. There's a solution to this. I know there is, something hovering in the shadows of my mind. It's only a matter of time before I can wheedle it out.

"What about Piper Fox?" he asks.

I frown at the abrupt change in conversation. "What about Piper?"

"Do you know anything about her?"

"Not really." And even if I did, I might not share it with Oliver. "She's a metalwork artist, and she lives in LA. Why are you interested?"

"I bought that gallery in SoHo."

"And?"

"Piper Fox does good work, but she's impossible to get ahold of. I want a show with some of her original pieces. Fit that into this deal."

I suppress a groan. Where is this coming from? I don't even want to know. Oliver is always like this, his thoughts and desires bouncing around faster than I can keep up with. More importantly, how can I work this to my advantage?

"How important would her art be to you?"

Maybe if Piper gives him some of her work, we can get him to compromise in some area. Not likely, but worth a shot.

"I know what you're thinking, and the camp is more imperative. We have a lot of work to do before we'll be able to open it, and while some of Piper's sculptures in my new gallery would be advantageous, it's not the top of my priority list. Her work is extremely rare right now, and you know how I like exclusivity."

"Okay. Well, I'll see what I can do."

We hang up, and I continue to sort through emails

and data Nora and our assistants have sent me over the past week, updates on some past businesses we've worked with, and paperwork for the current deals happening in Florida.

One of the emails from Nora, dated yesterday, says:

Are you done yet?

I hit reply.

No. But I'll see you in two weeks.

I check the calendar—it's less than that now. I frown. I was planning on being out of here by then and not coming back.

The thought sits like a stone in my chest. Not seeing Finley ever again doesn't feel like a viable option, but I don't belong here. I don't really belong anywhere.

I shove the self-defeating thoughts away and get back to work.

At midday, I take a break for lunch, grabbing a sandwich at a nearby restaurant.

After a few more hours of dealing with emails and phone calls, I get a text from Finley letting me know she's done, so I pack up my things.

There are only a few cars left in the parking lot when I arrive. Finley isn't waiting outside, so I park and go in. Too cold for her to wait out here, probably.

There's a middle-aged woman sitting in a booth when I make my way inside the front entrance.

"I'm here to pick up Finley."

She jerks her thumb down the hall. "She's using the rink. There's no game tonight."

"Thanks." My footsteps echo off the concrete walls. I emerge from the wide hallway into the arena. The stands are dark and empty, but the rink is lit up.

She's skating, alone, moving across the ice like she's flowing through water. Like a dancer. Like she owns the space. Quietly, I make my way down to one of the entrances to the ice and lean on the partition.

Her movements are smooth. She flies into the air, arcing and turning, and lands on one leg, the other leg stretched behind her as she spins. Her arms reach back, pulling her leg up nearly to her head.

Holy shit.

It takes my breath away. She's beautiful.

She told me . . . she said she was an okay skater. She was clearly not telling the complete story.

She glides over the ice, switching from forward skating to backward. My heart skips a beat when, with one smooth motion, a little dip, she's airborne, arms stretched above her. Her body blurs with spins before she lands smoothly on one leg and resumes flying over the ice with broad strokes of her legs.

Her eyes meet mine and widen. She shakes herself out of whatever trance she was in and skates over, coming to a neat side-stop in front of me.

I stare at her, speechless.

She shifts on her skates. "Sorry. Were you waiting long?"

I can't find words. I have no words.

She lifts a hand and snaps her fingers in front of my face. "Earth to Archer."

I blink.

"Um. Okay." She laughs nervously. "I need to grab my bag." She motions to the side and skates away.

What can I do but follow this intriguing, mysterious woman who continually knocks me for a loop?

By the time we make it to the car and I've stashed her bag in the back, I find my voice.

"Why didn't you tell me?" I turn the car on and glance over at her.

"Tell you what?" She buckles up, avoiding my gaze.

"Finley."

She fidgets in the seat.

"You are an amazing skater."

She sighs and then finally meets my eyes. "Was."

I blink. "What?"

"I *was* an amazing ice skater." She takes a big breath in and blows it out. "That time is over. Now I teach, and that is that." She clears her throat. "So what did you do all day?"

She's changing the subject and not subtly, but I let it slide. "Answered emails, made some phone calls." If she wants to be vague, I can do the same.

After a few blocks of silence, I glance over at her. I don't want to go back yet. I want to get her to open up, unravel some more of the mystery that is Finley Fox. "When was the last time someone took you to dinner?"

She shrugs. "It's been a while."

"Can I take you?"

She hesitates, and I wonder if it's been a while because she's strapped for funds. Everything they make goes back into the business.

"I'm paying." I grip the steering wheel one handed, hoping she'll agree, anxious that she won't. "I owe you since you cooked last night."

"I don't know."

"You can order the most expensive thing on the menu just to mess with me." I allow my lips to curve but keep my gaze fixed on the road, not wanting to see the denial on her face.

Her gaze on my profile is palpable. Finally, she speaks. "I would really like that."

I glance over, surprised, and she smiles at me. It's the first genuine smile she's given me since that first night—one that fills her whole face.

My chest squeezes. I didn't know until this moment that I had been waiting for that genuine happiness, aimed in my direction. I could conquer entire worlds for that smile. Or at least Oliver.

It's not the fanciest of eateries. We had to settle for somewhere that wouldn't sneeze at her leggings and my jeans and sweater, but it's nice enough, a family-style restaurant on the outskirts of town where you can order anything from burgers to seafood to pasta.

"You teach every week?" I ask once we're seated with our drinks in front of us. I want to know how she can skate like that, why she didn't pursue it as a career, and so many other things that I'm not entitled to.

She nods. "I wish there was a rink closer to Whitby."

I slide that information into place beside the other small bits of Finley I've managed to put together.

"Do your students know how good you are?"

She lifts one shoulder. "They are mostly aware—the older ones, anyway. Some of them have a lot of potential, but they need more time on the ice. It's a rough sport to have a career in."

"Is that why you never pursued one?" I attempt the question, bracing myself for her to avoid it.

She takes a sip of her wine and sets the glass gently on the table. "I did, actually. I competed from high school until I was twenty-two. But it wasn't meant to be."

"Why not?"

Her gaze dips to the table, and she takes a deep breath before answering. "When I was eighteen, I placed fourth in nationals. I missed the Olympics by one—they send the top three."

"Wow." I sink back against the padded booth seat.

"So four years later, I placed first in sectionals. I was considered a shoo-in for getting into the top three at nationals. But then Aria—" She presses her lips together, gaze shuttering.

My heart breaks for her. "When did she die?"

"A week before nationals." She meets my gaze. "They were together—Jacob and Aria were always together—when she died. It was a car accident. She was driving—without a license. I had to come home, of course."

"I'm so sorry. That she died, and what a shame you had to give up such a big dream. That's a tragedy on top of a tragedy."

She rubs the back of her neck. "My family is more important than skating. I would have given up all of that and then some to see Aria again."

I nod in understanding.

"The first few months after she died, none of us could believe it. Dad withered away once she was gone. He died a few years after Aria."

Her words click inside me, like a puzzle snapping into place, and the result is an image that's inherently familiar. "And you were left to pick up all the pieces."

Her eyes lift to mine. "I'm the oldest. I was eight when Mom took off, so I basically raised all of them except Mindy. Dad couldn't do it alone. But things got easier as we all got older. Then when Aria died, they were only fifteen. Taylor and Piper were still in high school. Mindy was off at college. She's only a year younger than me, but she had a scholarship to Vassar. I couldn't ask her to give that up to come home and take care of everyone."

"But you could ask it of yourself?"

"There wasn't a choice."

I frown, not liking the decisions that have been placed in front of her but understanding all the same. After all, my story is similar. I had to pick up all the pieces for Mom, because there was no other choice. I want to know more about her dad, about why her mom left, everything, but I don't want to pry. She's already shared more than I thought she would.

"Teaching is rewarding," she says. "I still get to skate, but in front of smaller crowds." She smiles. It's a tiny slant of her lips, but it's sincere. "It is gratifying, being a part of other people learning new skills, the joy, the freedom, the hope—passing it on. Besides, I'm too old now to be an Olympic hopeful."

"Really? You're barely thirty."

"I'm over thirty. There are fifteen-year-olds competing. I might as well be sixty."

I chuckle. "Despite your advanced age, watching you was . . . I can't even describe it. You were the most beautiful thing I've ever seen."

Surprise fills her eyes with warmth. "You need to get out more."

I grin. "That might be true."

The sense of awareness already pulsing in my chest expands, filling the space between us. It's the only explanation for why I share a piece of my past I hardly ever talk about. "My mom died when I was nineteen. She was my only family. It doesn't go away. The pain, the grief. It never goes away; it just changes shape." We share a look, connecting in mutual under-standing.

She reaches across the table and puts her hand over mine. "That's an amazingly accurate description. It's so true." Her hand squeezes mine. "I'm sorry about your mom. How did she die?"

The simple gesture lightens the dark edges around me. "She was sick most of my childhood." While the statement is true, it's not the full, unvarnished truth. My mother's illness is not a conversation to be had under the dusty lights of a casual-dining establishment while a kid with chocolate covering half his face stands in the booth next to us, hitting his dad in the head with a fork.

Of course, it's hard not to spill my guts out all over the table when her small hand is on mine. Her hands aren't soft and weak; they're strong and calloused from work. Real hands. I stare down at our fingers. When did we twine our fingers together? We fit. I don't have soft hands either. Although she is much smaller. I could hold four of her hands in one of mine.

"Even if you expect it, it doesn't make it any easi-er." Her voice is low, intimate.

"No. It doesn't."

Her thumb rubs over mine, shooting an electric spark up my arm. "What about your dad?"

It takes me a second to answer, even though I know she won't judge me. Childhood taunts ring in my ears nonetheless, schoolyard bullies who used to tease about how I must have done something to drive my father away. "He died. I never knew him or anything about him. He passed before I was born, according to my mom, but in hindsight, that could have been something she made up because she didn't know."

When I don't say anything further, she gives my hand one final press and then pulls back across the table.

I resist the urge to capture it back in mine, instead picking up my glass of water and taking a big gulp. "Tell me about Aria. What was she like?"

"She loved animals." Her smile is wistful. "She stole a mouse once from the school science lab that they were going to use to feed a snake."

I chuckle. "Did she get to keep it?"

She grimaces. "No, thankfully. But she did convince them to release the mouse back into the woods. After that, they waited until after her class to feed the snake."

We smile at each other, and then she continues. "Another time, when she was about five, we took a family road trip to Niagara Falls. We passed some roadkill and she started crying. She was inconsolable. She kept saying, 'Tell the deer to look both ways!'"

I laugh. "Sounds like she was a gentle soul."

"She really was." Her wistful gaze meets mine, and she grins. "She would have tried to keep that raccoon."

Our mingled laughter fills the air around table.

CHAPTER
Thirteen

FINLEY

Our food shows up, and we eat, the conversation flowing with ease.

"I talked to Oliver earlier today," he says.

I almost choke on my mashed potatoes. "You're going to tell me about it?" I take a drink of water to clear my throat.

"Yeah. Why not?" He dips a shrimp in cocktail sauce and pops it into his mouth.

"Aren't I the enemy?"

"We're not enemies. Maybe you and Oliver can be at cross-purposes, but I want to find a solution for both of you."

"If you say so. I still think it's impossible." I wave

my fork in the air. "But go ahead. What did my heinous archnemesis have to say?"

"Mostly more of the same. He's ready to buy, why can't I get you to capitulate, yadda, yadda, yadda. One interesting question came up, and in the interest of full disclosure, I wanted to let you know he asked me about Piper."

Surprise lifts my brows. "What? Why?"

"He bought a gallery. Sounds like he wants to feature some of her work."

I finish chewing before responding. "Everyone wants some of her work because her manager has made her super exclusive. He's also her boyfriend and a total ass."

His head tilts. "How so?"

"I don't even know how to describe it. He's controlling, but like over the top. It's like he's trying to cut her off from us. Or, I don't know, maybe she's cutting herself off. The last time we talked, I overheard him snap at her, and I told her he was out of line. Now she barely takes my calls."

"I'm surprised you haven't gone out there with your shotgun."

I laugh. "Trust me, if I thought it would help, I would."

Talking to Archer about everything . . . there's something about his calm manner and easy style that makes everything a little less bleak. I want to offer the same in return. I want to know more about his mom, but he didn't seem open to sharing.

"How did they meet?" he asks.

"Through her work, right after she moved to LA. At first, he was perfect, and she was so happy. He came home with her for Christmas when they first started dating, and everyone loved him. He's handsome, charming, and he treated her like a queen, in front of us, anyway, but . . . but we haven't really seen her since. There's always an excuse, and they're his excuses."

His eyes are sympathetic. "That's hard."

"It is hard." But something about sitting here, rolling around in all these deep feelings while he listens attentively . . . it makes it easier, the load a little less burdensome. "It's hard to talk to Piper about anything upsetting, you know? She's very sensitive, very sweet. Sometimes too sweet." I frown down at my half-finished meal.

"You miss her."

I lift my eyes. "I do, but I'm also wondering why Oliver brought her up to you. Is he stalking my whole family now?"

Archer winces. "Maybe?"

My mouth pops open. "Really?" My voice is high pitched.

"Not in a way where you have to contact the authorities," he rushes to assure me. "Oliver is a strange person, but he's not dangerous or anything. I wouldn't be surprised if he gathered a dossier with basic info on your family as soon as he decided he wanted the property. He's just very . . . goal oriented."

My brows lift. "You call that goal oriented?"

"It's hard to explain."

"Try me."

He smiles at my dry tone. "I've known him most of my life, and I still don't always understand the way his mind works. He's very one track, and he doesn't always get it when his actions are socially inappropriate, or maybe he just doesn't care." He rubs his chin, considering. "When he has an idea in his head of what he wants, he goes for it without thinking about anything other than reaching that goal."

"So he's Machiavellian."

"Sort of. He has scruples. It's just hard to find them sometimes."

I eat a few more bites of my steak before responding. "Well, I just hope he leaves Piper alone. One bad man in her life is enough. But enough about my sibling drama. What about you? Do you have any brothers or sisters?"

"Nope. I was an only child."

"Must be nice. All that peace and quiet."

"Actually, I always wanted siblings." His lips tilt in a rueful smile.

"Well, let me tell you what you missed out on: lots of arguing, teasing, and embarrassment. Not to mention the personal possessions going missing, fighting over food, and getting egged when you're making out with a boy for the first time." That last bit was courtesy of nine-year-old twin terrors.

He laughs and wipes his mouth with a napkin. "Honestly, that sounds like a blast to me. I would have loved to have someone to fight with. Even if it meant eggs on my face." His eyes drop to the table. "I was alone a lot."

He flags down a waitress while I pull pieces of my heart back together.

I only vaguely register his words as he asks for an order of baby back ribs to go, and the check.

"Late-night snack?" I ask once the waitress disappears and I find my voice again.

"No. I hear it's Jacob's favorite."

I blink in surprise. "It is."

"If he's out, you can stick it in the fridge for him."

I shake my head in amazement. "That's incredibly considerate of you to do for my asshole little brother."

"He's a good guy. He's just in a dark place."

The waitress returns with the check, letting us know the ribs will be ready in a few more minutes, and I excuse myself to go to the bathroom before we hit the road.

I wash my hands and stare at my reflection in the mirror, trying to imagine having no siblings, no family. Every time he lets it slip that he's alone, my heart breaks a little more. Obviously, he has friends, although if Oliver Nichols is an example of what his friends are like, no wonder he's lonely. I guess he has Nora, his business partner. It's not quite the same though, is it?

My family is a little broken, a lot damaged, and we probably fight too much, but we love each other. What would I do without them?

A few minutes later, everything is settled, and we're in the car, making the drive back to Whitby in comfortable silence.

We're nearly outside of town when I finally speak what I've been thinking about since we left the restaurant. "I'm sorry if what I said was insensitive, about my siblings and how they make me crazy."

"No. Not at all. I think it's one of those things where the grass is always greener. You know? If you don't have siblings, you want them, and if you have them, you want to get rid of them. Not literally, like"—he removes one hand from the wheel to make a neck-slashing motion—"but you know what I mean."

I smile. "Yeah. You're probably right."

We're silent the rest of the way to the cabins, lost in our thoughts while Archer navigates the winding road with ease.

He stops next to the truck at the side of the main house. At least Jacob is home. That means he and Frank didn't get into too much trouble.

"I have to run in and grab my things, anyway, so let me carry your bag to the door."

"That's not—" My protests are futile. He's out of the car before I can finish my sentence.

He grabs my duffle from the back and follows me to the side door.

"I can take it from here."

He nods and sets it on the stoop next to us. We should go inside. He needs to get his things and go back to his cabin, but then he'll leave, this night will be over, and I'm not in any hurry for this . . . whatever this is to end.

The porch lights are off, but muted light escapes through the windows and glass of the door. Wisps of canned laughter and voices filter into the air around us. No doubt Jacob fell asleep with the TV on again.

"Thank you for dinner and the ride and everything." My gratitude feels weak in the face of everything he's done today, not to mention the past couple of weeks.

"Of course."

We gaze at each other for a few long seconds that stretch into a minute.

I should go inside. Say goodnight. I've already said thank you, so there's no reason for us to stay out here together, and yet . . . I make no moves to go inside.

He steps a fraction closer. "What are we doing?" His voice is whispered, a secret shared in the shadows.

"We're just two friends, standing outside. Don't friends do that?"

The corner of his mouth lifts, a smudge of movement in the darkness. "I don't know. You stand around with all your friends, having intimate moments under the stars?"

"Maybe I want to." I can't look away from his shadowed face. What is he thinking? "But there are a lot of reasons why it's a bad idea."

"I'm leaving next week."

My heart picks up a dull, thudding beat in my chest. "Next week?" I can't stop the surprise from leaching into my tone.

"I have work to attend to in Florida. Before then, hopefully, we'll find a resolution for you and Oliver."

I can't even think about Oliver right now. Archer is leaving. I knew it was coming. Of course he can't stay here forever, but the thought still stings. It must be because I will miss the free labor. That's it: his ability to clean and work, not his easygoing nature, not his smile, not the way he listens or the way he's watching me now, with heat in his dark gaze.

"I'm glad that you came," I whisper.

"Are you?"

"I am. We're . . ." I fumble for words. "We're friends, right?"

"I would like that."

I nod. It's for the best. He's leaving. His life is elsewhere. He's rich, obviously attractive. He could have anyone he wants. Why the hell would he choose me? With my messed-up family, emotional baggage, and millions of obligations. I haven't been able to have any kind of real relationship, oh, you know, *ever*.

Archer steps back, shoving his hands into his pockets, regarding me from a safer distance.

I immediately miss his closeness.

What am I doing? I want him, but I can't risk it.

It sure feels like a good idea, here in the dark after a glass of wine, but how will I feel in the morning? How will I feel once he's gone?

I don't know. I already feel like I've lost.

We go inside. He gets his bag. We say goodnight, using pat expressions to avoid deeper feelings. I cover Jacob, who is passed out on the couch, then head upstairs to get ready for bed.

It's for the best. He's only been here a week, and he's already stolen all my righteous anger. Another week and he might crawl up into my heart and steal that too.

ARCHER

"Will you help me with cabin three?" Finley asks when I answer my door one morning, a few days after our dinner.

"Our happy honeymoon couple finally left?" I glance over at the cabin next door.

"Yes." She grimaces. "And they left behind a mess."

"Can't say I'm surprised." They were really going at in there. The groans and thumps broadcasted their activities every time I walked by.

We walk over to the cabin together, our arms brushing periodically, sending a flash of awareness through me with each accidental contact.

I expected things between Finley and me to be

stilted and awkward after our almost-kiss, but they're not.

If anything, we're more comfortable around each other than before—except for the ever-present tug of attraction. Okay, it's not a tug, it's a lightning bolt of electric tension, humming between us, growing in strength every time our eyes meet or fingers graze.

But I can't think about any of that because we're *friends.*

Once inside, I'm immediately assaulted by the smell of sex and stale food. Finley leaves the door open to air it out, even though it's a little chilly and overcast outside.

"Wow." Trash is scattered over almost every surface. The comforter is on the floor, and the sheets a tangle on the bed. One of the lamps has fallen over on the side table, the shade sitting on its side on the ground. "It looks like they had an epic party in here."

She wrinkles her nose. "Or an orgy." She snaps on some gloves and hands me a set, and we get to work.

I set the lamp to rights. "There were only two of them, right?"

"Yeah, but this is nothing. I've seen worse."

"Oh, yeah?"

She picks up an old banana and chucks it in a trash bag. "One time, a guest painted the entire toilet pink."

"Pink? Why?"

She shrugs. "Beats me. People do weird things. Another time, someone left some kind of glitter bath bomb in the tub. It took us forever to clean it out." She chuckles. "After trying to clean it up, Dad was showering twice a day, and we were still spotting glitter in his hair and behind his ears three weeks later."

I laugh and pull the sheets from the bed, exposing an entire box of condoms near the foot of the bed. I pick it up. "I think this is full." I peek inside. "Yep. A whole new pack."

"Here." She lifts her hands, and I toss it to her. She shoves it into the bedside drawer.

I lift my brows.

She shrugs. "Other amenities provided?"

We laugh, then a knock at the door has us both turning.

"Finley?" A dark-haired man in a suit stands in the doorway, one hand in a pocket.

I recognize him vaguely. Must have seen him around town.

"Hey, Reed." Her voice is overly bright.

"You've been avoiding my calls."

She sighs. "I know."

There's a tense silence. Reed glances over at me and then back at Finley.

I have no right to feel anything about any of this, but it doesn't stop the jealousy from curling through me anyway. Who is this man, and why is Finley avoiding his calls?

I try to catch her eye and find a way to wordlessly communicate if she needs me to get rid of him.

But she doesn't meet my gaze when she introduces us. "This is Archer. Archer, this is Reed."

"I'm Finley's ex-boyfriend." He delivers this statement in a matter-of-fact tone, followed by a smirk in my direction.

"Reed. Is that relevant?" Finley snaps.

"I don't know. Is it?"

She takes a deep breath before turning to me. "Sorry. I'll be right back." She walks to the door and stops in front of Reed. "Let's talk out here."

I stare at the open door after they've disappeared. I shouldn't care that he's her ex-boyfriend. He didn't say *boyfriend*; he most certainly said *ex*. Then why do I want to punch him in his stupid smirking face?

I shake myself from the thoughts. It's not my business.

I continue cleaning for what feels like an hour before allowing myself to check the clock. It's been two minutes. I keep going until I can't take it anymore, and then I grab the broom and move to the door—ostensibly to sweep the dust outside—and glance around.

They're talking over by a white Lexus. Must be Reed's. They're standing pretty close. I frown. Then he leans in and hugs her. Her arms lift, and she's hugging him back.

Envy grabs me by the throat. I turn away.

I'm sure it's nothing.

Ex-boyfriend.

I move away from the door before they catch me

spying and go to the bathroom to put all my frustration into scrubbing the bathtub.

Not much time has passed before Finley's footsteps herald her arrival.

"Archer?" she calls.

"In the bathroom."

I don't look up. I keep cleaning.

"Sorry about that."

I shake my head, keeping my gaze down. "Nothing to be sorry for."

It's silent except for the scrape of the brush against the porcelain. She doesn't move from the door. Her gaze is a tangible weight on me as I scrub.

Slow pressure builds between us, and there's no good reason for it. It's my fault. I have nothing to be jealous about. She's not mine. And she's not Reed's either. What is wrong with me?

"I'm overdue on property taxes," she says finally.

I go still then sit back on my knees to look up at her.

She's leaning against the door frame, arms crossed over her chest, eyes shiny. "Reed was helping me put it off as long as possible. He helped me challenge the assessment. Find ways to delay payment. But he can't help me anymore. I've got to pay everything that's due, plus the penalties, by next month. If I don't, they'll put a lien on it. I'm going to lose the property whether or not I sell to Oliver." Her eyes fall shut, tears tracking down her cheeks with the movement.

My heart breaks, knowing what this show of

vulnerability costs her. She's been so strong, so snarky and tough this whole time despite everything she's gone through.

I stand up and yank the dirty gloves off, tossing them into the tub before reaching out and tugging her into my arms.

She doesn't resist, slumping into me and pressing her face into my shirt, her arms wrapping tightly around my middle like she has to hold on or fall.

"I don't know what to do."

I rub her back, resting my chin on the top of her head, but I don't give her any platitudes. I know it wouldn't help.

Having her in my arms is glorious, even if these aren't exactly ideal circumstances. I rack my brains for ways to fix the problem.

"Would you take money from me if I offered it?"

"Absolutely not." She sniffs.

"Didn't think so."

She didn't even hesitate, and for some reason, the quick denial fills me with gratitude. I'm not sure I've ever met a woman quite like Finley Fox. I keep up the smooth movements up and down her back.

"What would Oliver say if he knew you offered me money?" she asks after a minute.

I chuckle. "He would not be happy."

I hold her and think about other ways to help her. What can I do? How can I make her smile again? She does too much. More than anything, she needs a break from all of this. The stress, the worry, a way to unwind and release the tension.

Of course, the first thought that comes to mind on how to release said tension involves me, Finley, a clean bed, and that giant box of condoms, but that isn't happening. I have to think of something else.

"I think you could use a day off."

She tenses in my arms, pulling back to look up at me. "A day off? Have you lost your mind? I have to fix this. I have to do something. I can't take a day off when everything is falling apart."

"It's exactly what you need to do. Sometimes, your brain needs a break. Your body needs a break. A problem that seems insurmountable won't be solved in a day. Almost everything works better after you unplug it for a few minutes. Even you."

"I don't know." Her eyes are uncertain when they meet mine. "Maybe."

I set her away from me. "Go get cleaned up and dress warm. I'll get Jacob to finish up in here. Meet me at my cabin in an hour."

She hesitates, worrying her bottom lip. "I don't think I can take a break. I don't even understand what that means. It's like a foreign language."

"You can, and you will. Trust me?"

She regards me, expression serious and hesitant. But finally, she relents. "Okay. Fine. Yes. I'll meet you in an hour."

Fifteen

ARCHER

"Where are we going?" She buckles up, tension still humming in the line of her shoulders.

A little over an hour has passed since we agreed to the day off. After running into Whitby for supplies, I meet Finley at my cabin and usher her into my still-running car.

"Not far. Just over the hill by the pond."

She glances into the back seat. "Are those axes? What's in the thermos?"

"Yes, those are in fact axes. The thermos has hot cocoa to keep us warm."

"Are you going to murder me?" She sags down in the seat. "I guess that's one way to solve all my problems. At least you want to get me warm first. You're a considerate murderer."

I chuckle. "You really keep your sense of humor through everything."

"I'm really good at using humor as a coping mechanism," she says drily. "It's a Fox family trait."

"Rest assured there will be no murder today. We'll be safe. We're going to do a little bit of axe throwing."

Her brows lift, and she grins. "Really?"

"Yep. Sometimes you just want to throw things. And throwing and stabbing at the same time is like an added bonus."

She laughs and claps her hands together, the taut line of her shoulders dropping an inch. "Okay. That sounds fun."

My heart lifts at her response. I wasn't sure how she would react to this idea. I doubt she's taken a day off in the past ten years.

The dirt road over the hill to the pond is rocky and rough from disuse. The SUV bobs and weaves, but we make it over without too much trouble.

I pull over next to a cluster of pine trees. Opening the trunk, I grab the four-foot pine board that I bought at the hardware store in Whitby, while Finley gets the axes from the back seat.

It takes me only a few minutes to set up the target in front of two trees set close together.

By the time I'm done, Finley's unpacking the rest of

the stuff I gathered, taking out folding chairs and setting them out along with a few wool blankets.

"What's in the cooler?" She tilts her head toward the item shoved into the back of the trunk.

I pick up the bundle of firewood next to it and toss it to the ground. "Wieners."

She grins. "We're going to roast wieners?"

"Yep." I squint up at the overcast sky. It's midday, but the sun is hiding behind clouds, the entire sky gray and dreary. "It's a little cold, so a fire seemed ideal."

"Fire and sharp objects." She nods. "I already feel better."

"Only one rule," I say.

She looks at me expectantly.

"There are no rules."

She rolls her eyes with a snort. "Okay. Whatever you say, *Fight Club*."

"Maybe one rule. Don't throw the axe at me."

She sticks out her bottom lip in a pout. "Party pooper."

I finish setting up the target, using spray paint to make a circle with an X in the center of the thick board.

"I have no idea how to do this," Finley says from behind me.

I turn around and shrug. "It's like darts, I guess, but with something a little bigger."

"Bigger is better." She covers her mouth with her hand. "Sorry. I'll try to keep the dick jokes to a minimum. I blame the wieners. They got into my head, and now they won't leave."

Laughter barks out of me. "This is your time. You make as many dick jokes as you need to. As long as they aren't at my expense, I'm good."

She presses her lips together as if she wants to comment on my nether regions, her gaze even dipping down slightly before returning resolutely to mine.

"Axes," I say with a determined nod. "Let's throw some axes."

I've never done this myself, but it doesn't stop me from showing Finley how to hold the axe, if only to get close to her and breathe in her scent just for a minute. We spend the next hour throwing axes at the board and hitting it a majority of the time. Finley is a quick study, and pretty soon, she's throwing better than I am.

When she finally hits the X I drew in the center of the circle, she jumps up and down, grabbing my arm. "I did it!"

"You did great."

She smiles up at me, but after a moment of us getting stuck in each other's eyes, she drops my arm and turns away. "So. Now can we roast some wieners?"

We get the fire going, and I pull out the hot cocoa and cups. She finds some long sticks for the hot dogs. We sit in chairs next to each other, sticking the dogs into the flames.

I don't want to bring up anything about the tax

issue, don't want to ruin the rest of her day, since the whole point of this is to not think about her problems —but I've been dying to know more about her relationship with Reed since he stood in the doorway and smirked at me. "So, how long were you and Reed together?"

She shrugs. "Off and on for around a year."

I clear my throat. "That's a decent amount of time."

She purses her lips in thought before she replies. "He's the one who broke it off with me. I'm always busy working, and he didn't like that I couldn't make him a priority."

Good. "His loss."

She spins the stick in her hand to cook the other side of the hot dog. "We were together but not really together, you know what I mean?"

"I can't say that I do."

Her mouth tips up on one side. "We weren't really . . . we didn't share much other than a physical relationship. I never felt really connected to Reed, like I could rely on him for anything more than friendship and, well, you know."

"Sex?"

She winces. "It sounds so crude. But yes. Even though we put the girlfriend and boyfriend labels on each other, which sounds so juvenile when you're over thirty. We didn't really have an emotional connection. It was more about alleviating occasional loneliness."

My head bobs. "I get it."

"What about you? Any relationship nonrelationships?"

"Not really. Even though it sounds sort of like we have a similar problem. I've been focusing on my business, which means I travel a lot."

"Lots of one-night stands?" Her tone is casual, but a muscle in her jaw tics.

I wince. "I can't say I've *never* done that, but only a couple of times. It's not really my thing." When the constant solitude was too much to bear on my own. "It's not as appealing as they make it seem on TV."

She nods.

"I've had a few short-term girlfriends, but it never seems to last. Like you, I've never been able to prioritize anyone, and relationships are work, I guess. I've never wanted to stay in one place long enough to give it a shot."

Until now. The thought strikes me like a hammer upside the head. I can't sit still. I get up and pull out the buns and condiments from the cooler with one hand, setting them on the lid and then dragging it behind our chairs to use as a makeshift table.

"Where do you live most of the time?" She opens the package of buns and hands me one.

It takes a few seconds for the ringing in my ears to ebb and for her question to register so I can answer. "I own a condo in Dallas, but I've been subletting it for the past year."

"Sounds like we are quite the pair of commitmentphobes." She puts her hot dog on her lap, clicking open the mustard. "What about your stuff? Like possessions? I think it would take a thousand years to clean out our house."

"I don't have a lot of personal items, just some things that belonged to my mother and photos and whatnot in a small storage unit in Dallas."

The dichotomy between us is interesting. I go everywhere and she goes nowhere, and yet neither of us has settled down, so to speak.

She takes a bite of her food and chews before asking, "Do you ever want to stay still for a bit?"

"I have to admit that it would be nice to have a home base." I hesitate before continuing. "I don't have any family, though, not like you. There's no one that depends on me or cares if I show up. Except Nora."

We're quiet for a minute, and Finley keeps casting me sidelong glances as if she wants to say something, but she's holding back.

"Go ahead. Ask whatever's rolling around in your mind." I gesture with my free hand, taking a bite of my hot dog.

"Why were you at that camp, the one where you met Oliver? You said your mother was sick a lot when you were growing up? What happened that sent you there?"

I consider how to answer her question, and she misinterprets the silence as avoidance.

"You don't have to answer."

"I know. I want to. It's a hard question. My mom was sick, but it wasn't that she was physically ill or anything. She had schizophrenia."

She turns, her knees leaning toward me. "Archer. I'm sorry."

"She was okay when she was on her meds. She was actually really intelligent in a lot of ways, very creative, but she couldn't work. She had a hard time with consistency, staying on task, or getting basic household things accomplished. We had a fixed income, and her medication made her tired a lot. She tried, she really did, but a couple of times . . ."

I pause, not wanting to bring this up, to drag the day down into my past problems, but Finley is watching me with those fathomless eyes, curious and sympathetic and nodding for me to continue.

I move my gaze to the flames flickering in front of us. "A couple of times, she stopped taking her meds because she thought she was better. She thought this time, she could stop taking them and it would be okay, but that's not how it works. One of those times, she took off for over a week. I was twelve. I had no food, no money. I snuck into the landlord's apartment to steal some peanut butter, and he called CPS when he realized I was alone. That's the summer I went off to camp."

"Archer." Her face is stricken, eyes wide, mouth open.

"It's fine." The phrase is rote, and it doesn't fool Finley.

She stands up and, without preamble, steps over to my chair and sits in my lap, wrapping her arms around me.

And suddenly, I'm not alone. Not anymore.

She presses her face into my neck, her nose cold against my skin, but the rest of her is a warm, sweet weight. I wrap my arms around her and hug her to me.

"It was okay. She got better. She got back on her meds eventually, although that was a nightmare by itself."

"Why?" The word is a warm puff of air against my neck.

"She lost her Medicaid and started self-medicating. Unfortunately, it's easier to get high than it is to get help. It took a while to get things sorted, for her to stabilize enough for them to send me home. She had no support system. No friends or family."

I squeeze her a little tighter, gathering the courage to continue.

"Eventually, we were reunited. I was lucky. I didn't have a terrible experience in the foster system. It wasn't ideal, but it could have been worse. And my mom loved me. She tried her best. Obviously, my childhood wasn't ideal, but there are so many kids who had it so much worse—including Oliver. Even though he never really opened up about his experiences, even to me, I heard enough to get the gist."

"I don't care about Oliver. I care about you."

My chest squeezes. "You do?"

She pulls back to look at me, one hand on my shoulder, the other in her lap. "Of course I do. And Oliver's experiences, even if they were worse, don't negate yours. That must have been terrible." Her gaze on mine is searching, waiting to see if I'll share more, but I don't. I reach for the hand in her lap and take it in mine and say nothing.

I don't want to talk about having to make sure Mom continued to take her meds, the terror that would grip me if she forgot, the continual anxiety of her slipping again, of ending up back in the foster system with families like the one Oliver got stuck with. Not to mention the fact that I had to start working at fourteen to make sure we could keep a roof over our heads and food in the fridge.

"You're a survivor." Her fingers squeeze mine.

"So are you."

She huffs. "I don't feel like a survivor. I feel like a flounderer."

I grin. "I don't think that's a word."

"It should be."

I tighten my grip on her hand. "You are a survivor. Jacob said you basically raised all of them."

She leans her head against my shoulder. "I guess that's true. But I had Dad and Mindy too. They worked just as hard."

"What about your mom? You said she left when you were eight?"

She shifts a little in my lap. "Only a year after the twins were born."

"What?" The knowledge knocks me back. "She left all of you, all six kids, with your dad?"

"Yep. Haven't heard from or seen her since. Dad didn't tell me until I was older, but she struggled with depression pretty bad, and having all us kids right in a row probably didn't help. She felt trapped by us, I think, even though she wanted kids so badly. She always wanted a big family, but then once she had it . . ." She shrugs.

"And you were so young when she left. Did you ever try to find out what happened to her?"

Her jaw flexes. "No. Dad did, I think, but he never told me anything. There might have been other things going on, but since we haven't seen her, and since Dad died, I don't know much."

"I'm sorry." I rub her back, wanting any excuse to touch her, even if it's a friendly pat. Although considering she is sitting in my lap, I'm not sure how platonic this is.

"My memories of her don't paint the best picture."

"Why do you say that?"

She leans back to meet my eyes. "Dad was an amazing parent. He would have done anything for us. He mortgaged the property the first time to pay for my ice skating lessons and choreography. I would never have made it as far as I did without him. He loved us with everything he had, did everything he could for all of us, and no matter how much we screwed up, we never doubted that fact."

"He died shortly after Aria?"

"Yes. He never quite recovered. Then he was diagnosed with prostate cancer and . . . he just withered away." She swallows. "I wouldn't have gotten through that time without Jacob. He took over most of Dad's care."

"So much loss."

We're silent for a moment, sitting there, breathing. After a minute, she speaks. "You know, I don't know if I ever really dealt with any of it. After Aria died, I was busy taking care of Dad and the rest of the family plus keeping the business alive. I just threw myself into trying to fix everything and never really stopped to process."

"Sometimes we do what we have to to survive."

Her eyes search mine. "I suppose you understand that better than most."

"Grief is universal. No one is immune."

She blows out a breath. "I was lucky to have him while I did. Mom was very erratic. If we had ended up with her or if she had stayed and they had just divorced or something, it might have been worse. I knew some kids whose parents split and shared custody, and it was rarely amicable. A lot of times, the parents would use the kids against each other."

Something about the words "shared custody" worms into my mind and blends with the thoughts and ideas that have been swirling there over the past week.

Shared custody.

And then it clicks into place.

Oliver and Finley could form a shared partnership.

"How did you get this scar? I keep meaning to ask." Her finger traces over my eyebrow.

"Bar fight."

Her eyes widen. "Really?"

I chuckle. "No. I ran into a swing set."

She laughs. "The bar fight story is better."

A drop of cold water hits my forehead. Then another falls on Finley's cheek.

Her head drops back as she examines the sky above us.

"Rain."

As if the word summons the deluge, the sky opens up.

She yelps and leaps from my lap.

Together, we grab the chairs and food and put them back in the car.

I throw the cooler back into the trunk and then make sure the fire gets completely put out and we haven't left behind any trash. We leave the targets behind—I can get them later—but everything else gets packed up, and we make it back over the hill before the road turns into a muddy mess.

We're silent on the short drive. I'm not sure what Finley's thinking, but my thoughts are whirring through possibilities and ideas. I pull up to the side door of the main house to drop her off.

"Thank you. I had a great time. I'll see you tomorrow?" She searches my face.

I nod. "Yes. See you tomorrow." Then I wait while she runs inside. I want to follow her. I want to have the right. Despite how much we've shared, I can't even consider it, not unless she makes the first move. But it's getting harder and harder to resist, to keep my feelings inside and my hands to myself.

Once the door is shut, I head back to my cabin.

My mind is still weighing and considering the ramifications of getting Oliver and Finley to split the property. We could turn it into a camp, like Oliver wants, but Finley could stay and help manage it. With a lot more help, obviously.

Of course, there's always the distinct possibility that neither will agree or budge on this. They're both stubborn and set in their ideas. I'm not sure if it will give Finley exactly what she wants, but it's a step in the right direction.

The only thing is, once I put this idea out there, if Finley likes it, I'll have no reason to stay. The thought is like an axe to my burgeoning hope. It might be for the best anyway. The more I'm around Finley, the more I want her, and the harder it is to keep a friendly distance.

FINLEY

I swipe to answer the phone as soon as the name appears on the screen. "Piper." My voice is high pitched—overly enthusiastic. She rarely calls, so when she does, it's hard to tamp down my excitement.

"Hey, Finley. Just checking in on you and Jacob. It's been a while." Her voice is quiet, wan, and tired.

"We're doing great!" If great means losing our home, Jacob turning into a nonfunctioning alcoholic, and falling for the enemy. "How are you doing?"

"I'm fine." But her voice is flat.

"That's good. That's really good. It's snowing like crazy here." I lean back in the office chair and turn my gaze toward the front window. Overnight, the temperature dropped and the rain turned into snow. It's been coming down ever since, chunky flakes flurrying to the ground, the thick blanket growing taller by the hour.

"I miss the snow." Her tone is more longing than one might expect considering we're discussing the weather.

Worry jabs at me. "You can come home any time you want. You know that. You could come home for Easter. Or you could fly home today and play in the snow."

She sniffs. "Listen, Finley, I—" A door slams in the background. She covers the receiver with a hand and speaks to someone, her voice too low for me to make out the words.

"Piper? Is everything all right?"

"It's fine. I have to go. I'll call you later."

"Wait, please. If there's something going on—"

"Everything is fine." The response is quick and firm, if rushed.

"Okay, okay. You can always"—my mind scrambles —"if you need anything and you can't say it, use a safe word."

At that, she releases a low chuckle. "And what would that be?"

"I don't know . . . rutabaga."

She doesn't laugh. It's quiet on the line.

I keep going. "Say the word, and I'm on the next flight to California, and I'll do whatever you need, whatever you want. Just say the word." I'm practically begging. It's the truth. I would do it. I would run up another credit card, sell the truck, burn the world to the ground to get to Piper and keep her safe.

Ben's voice murmurs in the background. Then Piper says in a voice that's too calm, too dead. "Everything is fine. I'll call you later."

The line disconnects, and I want to throw my cell phone across the room—and I would if I actually had the money to replace it.

I take a few deep breaths instead, but it's not nearly as satisfying.

According to Piper, it's always fine. But it's not okay, not at all. And there's nothing I can do about it. I'm completely helpless. Frustration pounds through me. She's across the country. If something happened, I would never forgive myself. It would be like when Aria died, and I wasn't there.

My heart threatens to break apart.

But what can I do? There's nothing I can do or say to make her leave Ben, to make her come here. All attempts to force her will lead to her pulling away further.

How do you convince someone to change their life? How do you convince them there's a problem in the first place?

I don't know how much time passes. I stare blankly at the calendar on the computer. A few last-minute cancellations have come through, and I'm glad for it. The last thing I want to do is go around cleaning and prepping rooms.

I should check that all the heaters are on enough so things don't freeze in the empty cabins. But I don't want to move. I don't want to do anything.

I'm still sitting there when the front door opens and Jacob stomps in, shaking snow from his boots and coat. "We cleared off the drive with the snowblower."

"Everyone canceled."

"Everyone?"

I gesture at the computer. "Well, all two of our reservations for today."

"That's a bummer. I'm sure we can use the money."

"Yeah, about that . . .we should talk." *While you're still sober.* I didn't tell him yesterday. Maybe I should have, but I didn't want to lose the glow I had from being with Archer despite the heavy topics we covered. I also didn't want the added stress giving him an excuse to drink. Might as well tell him now, when there are no guests around and he's already cleared up the driveway.

He puts his coat on the rack and then sits in the chair across from me.

"We owe some back taxes to the county."

He blinks a few times. "What does that mean?"

"It means we could lose the house if we don't come current."

His brow furrows, eyes full of confusion. "Can we pay it? Can we get the money from somewhere?"

I shake my head. "No. We don't have it."

He stands, hands clenching. "That can't be right. We can't lose our home. There has to be a solution."

"I've already tried everything. Reed even helped me over the past year to put it off as long as we could."

His hands tunnel through his hair. "How could you let this happen?"

My mouth drops open. How could *I*? "It's not like I'm choosing any of this, Jacob. I've done everything I can."

But have I? His words pulse through me, along with all my worst thoughts about myself, everything I've worked against since Aria died. No matter what I do, no matter how hard I work myself to the bone, it's never enough. I can't fix anything.

"Have you though? How has this place been in our family our whole lives, and now that you've taken over, it's gone downhill?"

It's not me he's angry at, it's the situation. At least, that's what I try to tell myself. I've kept too much from him, and now it's time to come clean. "Dad mortgaged the property when we were kids to help raise us. To pay for my ice skating, to finance Mindy's education. Then he did it again when he got sick to pay his medical bills."

He sits back down, his elbows on his knees, his hands covering his face briefly. "Why didn't you tell me?"

"I didn't know until after he died, and I didn't want to worry you."

His jaw clenches, and he turns away. "If you had mentioned it sooner, I could have helped."

"Maybe. Maybe not. This is where we are though."

He blows out a breath. "How much time do we have?"

"We have to pay by the end of next month, or they'll put a lien on it."

He's silent, staring at the corner of the desk. I glance over, but there's nothing there.

"Is this why Archer's leaving?"

The words hit me like a physical blow. "Archer is leaving?"

He waves a hand, unconcerned. "Yeah, I guess."

"What? When?" Panic squeezes my throat, making my voice high and thin.

"Soon." He shrugs. "He said he was going to pack after we were finished." He stands up again and heads toward the interior door. "I need a drink."

I want to run after him. I want to scream out my frustrations. I want to tell him he needs to stop acting like a child and grow the hell up. Archer has done more for this place in two weeks than he has in three years. The last thing he needs is a drink. But I've been down this road. I've tried cajoling, bribing, yelling. It doesn't make a difference. If anything, it will become an excuse to drink more. I can shout and cry until I'm blue in the face, and it won't change his behavior.

I don't have the strength to get into it with him. Not right now.

I have other pressing thoughts that are clamoring to be heard.

Archer's leaving. He said in a week. It hasn't been a week yet.

Was he even going to say goodbye? The thoughts burn through my already emotionally heavy morning and turn all my stress and anxiety into fury. I can't believe he's leaving. He doesn't have to be in Florida until next week. Why would he go? Why didn't he say anything?

I grab my coat and slam out the front door, marching through the blizzard, the flakes falling faster, obscuring my vision, the cold air cooling my heated face. I'm surprised steam isn't shooting out of my ears and melting the snow.

I squint through the blowing snowflakes. His car is still here.

Striding up the porch steps, I bang on the door. It swings open immediately.

"Finley."

It would be easier to hold on to my rage if he didn't look entirely lickable and didn't say my name in that rumbly, sexy voice. His cheeks are pink from being out in the cold. He's wearing jeans and boots, a coat opened in the front, the snug thermal underneath visible. His suitcase is opened on the end of the bed, half full.

"You're leaving?" I stomp inside then spin around to face him.

He closes the door.

I cross my arms over my chest, holding my anger and indignation around me like a cloak.

"Are you coming back?"

He doesn't answer right away, and the silence is submerged in friction.

My heart thuds a dull beat in my chest, my stomach twists.

"It's for the best."

I pace away. He's too close. "No."

I stare down at his open suitcase, noting the neat packing, everything cleaned and folded with meticulous precision. That's so like him.

"No?" His expression is confused. Even his perplexed face is adorable and endearing. I avert my eyes. If I look at his face while he tells me he's leaving forever, I might end up punching him.

"You can't leave."

"I can't?"

"You can't come here and be all," I gesture at him, "like this! Then leave and expect me not to get upset about it." I stomp my foot.

The corner of his mouth tips up.

I stalk over to him and point at his face. "Don't you smile at me. This isn't funny."

He grabs my finger in a gentle grip. "I think it's sort of funny." His voice is low and amused. He tugs my finger toward him, forcing us closer.

"Just tell me why," I insist.

His head dips, and his fingers lace with mine.

My lips part, anticipation pulsing through me. Will he kiss me now?

When he speaks, he's so close, the words puff against my lips. "Because I can't handle being around you and not touching you like I want to. Like you're mine."

My stomach flips.

I clench his hand, his large, talented hand. A hand that can fix things, show the most soothing care . . . and deliver amazing orgasms.

I lean in and press my mouth to his.

He doesn't hesitate or freeze. This kiss is nothing like our first. There's no shock, no indecision. As soon as our mouths touch, his arms surround me, hauling me against him.

CHAPTER
Seventeen

I shrug off my coat without removing my mouth from Finley's. Her hands slip under my thermal, tracing my stomach before tripping over my back.

Her fingers are cold, but I'm on fire everywhere, craving more of her skin against mine. Every cell in my body exalts in the feel of her in my arms, what I've wanted ever since the night I first touched her, first tasted the sugary sweetness of her skin.

I pull back for a second to push her coat off her shoulders. It falls to the floor, and our mouths meet again, nipping, sucking, our tongues meeting and sweeping against each other in a clash of pent-up desire.

I shove my suitcase out of the way. It crashes onto the floor with thumps and clatters.

I nudge her onto the bed, crawling over her so I can trace the lines of her face, revel in the sensation of her body beneath mine.

"Archer." She reaches for me, pulling my hips against hers.

I don't want to rush this. I need to hold back, relish each moment and enjoy every second I get to keep my hands on her, but the blood is rushing through my body like a freight train of desperate need.

She pulls my head down, her tongue pushing past my lips with a moan, hips tilting against mine. Her enthusiasm ignites my own, forcing it to burn brighter, hotter, more demanding. She jerks my shirt up and off and then runs her fingers over my chest, caressing the smattering of dark hair, tracing it downward with a finger.

Braced over her, my arms shake with restraint.

"Finley."

"Hmmm." Her eyes are cast downward, where she's plucking at the button of my jeans.

"I need to feel you. Your skin. Everything."

We pull her shirt over her head and then collide in a tangle of limbs, our lips seeking. She has a bra on, but I can't bring myself to pull away long enough to snap it off. I never want to let her go.

We kiss and caress, hands roving, mouths teasing, for long moments. Then, suddenly, she pulls back.

"Wait. Wait," she says, her breath catching as I suck on the delicate skin of her neck.

"What?" I brace myself over her again.

"Do you have a condom?" She's panting, staring up at me, lips pink and swollen.

My brain takes a minute to register the words. Condom? Condom. *Shit.*

"I don't have any." I glance around as if one might magically appear nearby. I didn't think I'd need any, I hoped, of course, but never imagined . . .

But I have seen condoms recently.

Our eyes meet in a clash of shared memory.

"Cabin three," she says.

"They were there yesterday. No one but Jacob has been in there since."

She winces. "I really don't want to know if he took them."

"I'll go get them." My hungry gaze roves over her, dark hair falling in messy layers around her shoulders, her breasts heaving underneath a pink bra—I've never experienced such violent thoughts against fabric. "The last thing I want to do is put clothes back on you."

"The feeling is mutual." She runs her hands over my shoulders, inciting a full-body tremble.

Swallowing, I make a herculean attempt to pull my thoughts out of neanderthal and up to higher functioning. "I'll run and grab them." I push away from her and stand up, taking a deep breath, running my hands through my hair, before making my way to the door only through supreme force of will.

"Wait."

I turn around. Her eyes trail over me, snagging on my unbuttoned jeans. "You're going out there like that?" She licks her lips.

The last thing I want to do is leave her for even a second, but I have little choice.

"I'll go quick." Faster than I've ever moved in my life, most likely.

"I'll go with you."

My brows lift. "Like that?"

She lifts a slender shoulder. "No one is around, and we match."

A grin spreads my cheeks. "Okay."

She bounces off the bed and meets me by the door. I guess it's a good thing we haven't removed our shoes yet.

"Ready?"

She nods and grabs my hand.

I open the door, and we run through the falling snow, holding on to each other, shrieking and laughing like idiots.

The other cabin is cold and dim. I race over to the side table and open it, pulling out the box and shaking it. Still full. *Thank God.*

"Got 'em."

She's standing near the door, her arms wrapped around her bare midriff, shivering.

I glance around. "We could stay here."

"All I can think about is how many times that couple had sex on probably every surface. Plus it's freezing."

"All excellent points." My own mind is devoid of all rational thoughts. All that remains are thoughts of how I want to be inside her as soon as possible. "Let's go."

We run outside, breathless and cold, gripping each other.

In the center of the snowstorm, I come to an abrupt halt, tugging Finley back against my chest and lowering my mouth to hers. I brush my lips against hers, catching the snowflakes that settled there. Her fingers are cold on my back as she presses closer. Her mouth opens against mine, the heat of her tongue a stark contrast to the blowing snow.

I don't want to let her go, but we need to get inside.

I release her with a groan.

Once we're back in the warmth of my cabin, I toss the condoms onto the side table and push Finley back on the bed. "Let me warm you up." I snap off her bra.

She giggles. "You're going to warm me up by removing more clothing?"

My mouth covers one of her breasts, and she gasps and arches up into me, her hands sliding into my hair.

Our jaunt through the winter wonderland outside did nothing to calm the raging lust galloping through my body.

It's been too long, and Finley is too sweet, too incredibly soft underneath my fingertips. Once I'm inside her, it won't take much for this encounter to come to an end. With that in mind, plus the hunger pounding inside me compelling me to bring her endless pleasure, I move down her body, trailing my lips down her stomach. Reaching her pants, I tug them down her legs, chucking them to the side along with her underwear.

Then I settle between her strong thighs, running my hands down to her calves and then back up, smoothing my palms over her skin and taking my time, breathing in her scent, my mouth watering in expectation.

"Archer." My name is a groan leaving her mouth. She arches her hips toward me, seeking relief.

I don't make her wait. I start with delicate kisses, brushing my lips against her, rubbing my mouth back and forth, up and down. Gradually, I increase the pressure as her moans get needier and her hands grip my hair harder, her legs flexing and tilting underneath me.

I love the taste of her, the little noises she makes, the way her hips shift under me and her hands clench in my hair. I pull her to the brink of the abyss with kisses, nips, and finally long, lingering licks. Her cries grow in volume and cadence, and then I slip a finger into the heat of her. I reach my free hand up her body, rubbing her nipple with my thumb, and then she goes rigid, arching and bending.

Her body seizes, shaking and shuddering. I keep up

the ministrations but ease up slightly, riding it out as the orgasm rolls through her body and she slumps back against the bed.

My body is about to spend right along with her. I don't want to let go until I can get inside her. The craving to have her heat surrounding me is beyond intense. Logical thought has fled. I'm a mass of need, pure animal instinct pounding in my head and in my cock, craving the relief she can provide. I need her more than I need air to breathe.

Fumbling, half out of my mind, I shake out a dozen condoms, and they fall all over the side of the bed, scattering on the bedspread, some of them tumbling to the floor. I grab the closest one and rip it open with my teeth, moving back between Finley's legs and sliding it on before pushing into her.

"Oh my God."

She's tight, wet, warm, and mine. She smiles up at me, sleepy and satisfied, her arms wrapping around my neck, drawing me down for a kiss while I plunge inside her again and again, my movements increasingly erratic as the building pleasure reaches an inevitable conclusion.

"Finley," I moan into her mouth, wanting this to last longer but knowing there's no way I can stop it. Not this first time. I really hope she lets me make it up to her.

She kisses my jaw, trailing her lips over to my ear, nipping at the lobe. "I love the feel of you inside me."

The words are a palpable stroke of her lips, and that's all it takes to push me into the longest, most gratifying, most forceful orgasm that's ever spun through my body.

When I come back to earth, I'm lying on the bed on my side. Finley is snuggled into my chest, one of her hands tracing over my shoulder.

"Wow," I say.

She pulls away far enough to meet my gaze with a shy smile. "Yeah."

"I promise I'll last longer next time." I wince. "Maybe the third or fourth time."

Her responding smile is bright and instantaneous. "I loved that you wanted me so badly."

"I still do." I nip at her chin, and she laughs.

Cupping her face in my palm, I trace her cheek with a careful touch then thread my fingers into the hair at the base of her head to hold on while I kiss her.

It starts out slow, sweet, and gentle, but within a minute, my body stirs.

"Again?" she says, her gaze dipping between us to where my erection is waking up and nudging her thigh.

"And again, and again," I whisper back and then roll onto my back, dragging her on top of me.

CHAPTER
Eighteen

FINLEY

I blink my eyes open, awareness leaching in slowly. The room is entrenched in soft darkness. I sit up in the bed and glance around. The clock on the nightstand reads five thirty.

The fireplace is lit, embers casting a soft glow. I'm in Archer's cabin. Cabin four. I think from now on, I will always think of it as his. As ours.

God, today was amazing. I flop back against the bed as memories flood through me, making my limbs tingle along with my slightly sore nether regions. My eyes fall shut as I conjure the exact moment he tugged his shirt off. I finally got to get my hands on his large, powerful, and well-developed chest, something I'd fantasized about every time my gaze was drawn to the play of muscles flexing under his shirt.

But he's more than just a handsome face and strong body. Archer is exactly how I pictured he would be in bed: considerate, caring, completely in tune to my needs and what would make me satisfied while also making me feel wanted and desired. Like when he shoved his meticulously packed luggage onto the floor, not caring that everything went flying everywhere or the fact that there was another perfectly fine and empty bed a few feet away. The way he looked at me. The hunger in his gaze, the care in his touch. Just thinking about it makes me want him all over again.

After the first two frantic lovemaking sessions, the third time was slow and sweet. He stared into my eyes, carefully monitoring every reaction, every time breath caught in my throat, every uncontrollable moan, interspersed with deep, wet kisses.

I sigh and sit up again. Where is he?

Trepidation slithers through me. What if he changed his mind? I clutch the sheet to my chest. Are his things still here? What if he decided to leave? What if all of this was—?

The doorknob jiggles, and the door swings open.

Relief gusts through me.

His grin is dazzling, gaze tracking over me with open admiration. "You should wear that forever."

A startled laugh escapes me. "This sheet?"

"Yes." He lifts the paper bags in his hands, kicking the door shut behind him. "We needed sustenance."

I'm so happy he's here, I'm almost lightheaded. Or maybe it's the smell of food, since I haven't eaten since this morning. My stomach growls.

It's almost frightening how much he's come to mean to me in such a short time. And he's still leaving. Isn't he? I don't get to keep him.

I should ask. I should bring up all the things still between us, but I can't ruin this time together.

"Jacob is home safe. He left the side door wide open though, and your kitchen was freezing."

I groan and cover my face with one hand.

"Don't worry. It's all taken care of now."

"Thank you."

"I also brought burgers from the diner in town and snacks for sustenance. I need you to keep up your strength." He walks closer, setting the bags on the bed and leaning over to drop a kiss on my head.

I smile up at him. "Do you? And why is that, pray tell?"

He shrugs. "No particular reason." He sits next to me, kicking off his shoes.

I open the bags and take out Styrofoam containers, checking each one. The larger ones have burgers and fries, and a smaller one has a big slice of chocolate cake. One of the other bags is full of bottled water.

"It's important to stay hydrated," he says when I hand him one.

I pop a fry into my mouth. "How are you so perfect?" I grumble.

"You say that like it's a bad thing." He scoots back on the bed, opening his food container on his lap.

"It kind of is. What's wrong with you?"

He considers the question. "I squeeze my toothpaste from the top."

I gasp. "Psychopath."

"I also put milk in a bowl before the cereal and eat Kit Kats on the horizontal without breaking them apart."

"That's it. I'm out of here." I make like I'm going to get out of the bed, and he laughs and tugs me back down, the sheet pooling around my hips.

Archer hisses in a breath between his teeth, his eyes heated and greedy.

"The rest of the food can wait." His voice is a caress that I feel low in my belly, his eyes fixating on me as my container of food gets shoved onto the table.

His clothes get yanked off and flung away, my body going warm and liquid with arousal as each part of him is exposed. How can I crave him again so soon, so intensely?

I push on his shoulder, and he flops back, lips parted, eyes heavy lidded as I crawl over him, grabbing for one of the condoms scattered around the bedspread.

His fingers trail up my body, cupping my breasts. One hand glides downward, coming to a rest between our bodies, his thumb rubbing against the bundle of nerves at the apex of my thighs.

"Archer," I breathe his name in and out.

I can't wait anymore. I rip open the condom and get up on my knees to sheathe him before sliding back down, loving the way he fills me, the way he watches me, the way his hands worship and arouse.

We move together, gasping and shifting. I lean over to kiss him, his tongue thrusting into my mouth in time with his hips. Pleasure spirals and twists through me, through him, his chest shaking under my hands as we climax together, shuddering and shaking and shattering as one.

I slump on top of him, boneless and satisfied, his fingers drifting through my hair.

"Let's never leave this bed," I mumble.

He chuckles, the sound a rumble in my ear. "Those terms are acceptable. But let's shower first."

But first, we finish eating dinner, leaving the chocolate cake for later. The food is cold, but who cares? It tastes better than anything I've ever eaten. After the shower, during which I spend an inordinate amount of time washing all of my favorite spots on his body— which takes a while—we get back under the covers. In the darkness, lying face to face, we speak in whispered tones about nothing of major importance. Just mundane things, like his favorite color is purple, mine is blue. His favorite movie is *The Princess Bride*, and mine is *Ever After*. We debate whether *Grey's Anatomy* or *Chicago Med* is better and where to find the best pizza in the city.

I want to know everything about him, all the little things and the big things. It's scary and thrilling, and when we share the chocolate cake, it's also arousing.

Especially when Archer spreads some of the chocolate frosting on my skin and cleans it up with his mouth.

I've never felt this way about anyone, ever. Granted, it's not like I've had a ton of experience or partners, but with Archer, everything is . . . effortless.

One thought lingers as I descend into slumber.

I wish I could keep him.

I wake up in early-morning light with one arm wrapped around my waist and a large palm cupping my breast with gentle possession. Archer's breath tickles the back of my neck, and a thick rod of heat presses against my back.

Considering the number of times we've had sex in the past twenty-four hours—I think we got halfway through that condom box—I can't believe he's still aroused.

His hand moves, his thumb tripping over my nipple, and I arch back against him as heat floods through my body.

Damn.

I can't believe *I'm* still aroused.

"Finley." His voice is a sleepy growl that vibrates through my back and flows out and down, igniting fire through my limbs.

I stretch away from him to grab for the box of condoms.

"Again?" Now his voice is tired and amused. His palm flattens down my spine, smoothing over my skin. "Are you sure you're not too sore?"

"Not yet." I turn around with a condom in hand, reaching for him. "Not even close."

Thirty minutes later, I'm half asleep, sprawled on top of him, my ear pressed to his chest, lulled by the beat of his heart and his slow, easy breaths. His fingers trail circles over my upper back.

"I have an idea that might help you save this place."

I lift my head, yanked immediately out of my drowsy stupor.

His brows furrow. "We don't have to talk about it if you don't want. I don't want to upset you or ruin this time together, but I have to tell you."

I scoot up and rub my nose against his to make him smile again before pulling back. "You won't ruin it. Unless all the sex was a part of some ruse to get me to relent to Oliver's deal in exchange for a whole lot of sex. In which case, it's working."

He chuckles and brushes a kiss against my lips. Then another. And another. Then he licks into my mouth, one hand meandering down to my waist to shift me closer, his hips twisting to press his erection right *there.*

I hiss in a sharp, aroused breath. "Wait." I lean back. "Archer. You were going to tell me your idea."

He blinks at me. "Oh. Right. Sorry. It's really easy to be distracted when you're naked."

"Here." I cover his eyes with my hand.

He palms my right butt cheek. "I can still feel you."

"I can move away."

"No, no, I got this." He blows out a breath and removes my hand from his face, holding it against his chest. "What if you and Oliver split ownership in the property?"

"What do you mean?" My heart picks up a rapid beat in my chest.

Shared? I don't even know what to think about such a thing.

"You would still live here, in the main house, with Jacob. You would still own half the property, but instead of running the cottages, you could help manage the camp, maybe?" His brows lift in question. "Oliver would have input on the details, of course, and he would provide the capital for the rebuild, any staffing needs, and cover the expenses of whatever else needs to be done. You could manage staff, help with the kids, whatever you want. I would make sure you have a choice over how much or how little you want to be involved."

I stare at him while the idea twists and twirls in my mind. Retain half ownership? It's better than nothing. If I don't do anything, I'll lose the whole property, but . . . help manage a camp for kids? It's not something I've ever considered.

Archer is watching me back, his eyes careful, apprehensive.

"It's not a bad idea," I say finally. "I'm not opposed to it. I don't know how I think about having to work with the devil of New York City, but it's better than losing the property completely, either to Oliver or to the county." I rest my chin on his chest, breathing in his scent. "I guess I don't really know what to think."

He smooths back my hair. "You don't have to think anything yet. I haven't mentioned anything to Oliver. I wanted to let you simmer in it. Think about it before I approach him."

"You really think he'll go for it? It sounds like he's getting the short end of the stick. He has to front all the money for everything."

He chuckles. "For Oliver, money isn't the concern. This will be a tax write-off for him anyway. Plus, it will get him the result he wants, although sharing will be difficult. For him more than you. He is like a toddler."

"How did you guys even become friends? You said before you had to help each other against some bullies or something?"

He's tense and silent for a second before he replies. "Yeah. I think I mentioned how Oliver tried to fight me at first. He was an angry boy. Most of the kids were. And he was always hungry." He stops, hesitating for a second before continuing in a lower voice. "I got the sense his foster family would withhold food as punishment, as a means to get him to cooperate. Amongst other things."

I gasp. "Holy shit. That's terrible." I don't want to feel sorry for Oliver, my enemy, but knowing this background . . . my heart breaks for any child in such a hellish situation.

"He would hide food under our bunk bed, in the bathroom, wherever he could hide it."

I wince. He was just a boy who experienced such scarcity in childhood he felt the need to hoard food. Maybe that was why he's so rich; his hoarding didn't really change, it just shifted from food to . . . everything.

Archer continues the story. "One night, I heard him sneak out, and I followed. He went to the kitchens to get more, but another group of boys was there waiting. There were three of them. Two held him back while the third hit and punched him. He was small, but what he lacked in size he made up for in stubborn fury. Anyway, I had followed him and was able to intervene. After that, those boys left us alone. The next year, we made another friend, Mason, and it was the three of us against the world. We only had each other."

I bite my lip, watching him. "And despite all of that, you're not going to tell him about how I owe taxes? If he waits a month, he could have the whole thing without me and at a lower cost."

"No. I'm not telling him."

My brows lift. "Even though you are lifelong friends who went through hell together?"

"He sent me here so he can open his camp. That's what I'm giving him. I also promised you I would find a solution that would work for both of you, and I don't break my promises. I understand why your home is so important to you. Your father's memory, Aria's memory, your family history, they all live here. You have something I would never want to take away from anyone. I would never do anything to hurt you. You know that, right?"

"I know." My throat grows tight. His words make my eyes sting, but I don't want to examine these feelings too closely, so I ask another question. "You really think you can convince him this is the best deal?"

"I can try."

"When are you going to talk to him?"

"I think it's a discussion best had in person. After I'm done in Florida, I'll come back to New York and talk to him then."

I sit up slightly, my hands still resting on his chest. I keep my gaze on his chin. "And then what?"

"What do you mean?"

I swallow. "I mean . . . will you come back here?"

His fingers brush my chin, tipping my face up to

meet his gaze. "Do you want me to come back?" His voice is almost a whisper, his gaze probing.

I scoot up, lifting off his chest slightly so that I can reach out and hold his face in my hands, enjoying the feel of his scruff on my palms. "I want you to come back. At least for a little bit? For as long as you want."

His responding grin is blinding. "I want to come back," he says. "I will come back."

And then his mouth presses against mine, and he promises me with whispered words and soft kisses and every caress of his hands.

CHAPTER
Nineteen

The next week passes quickly. Archer and I continue to work together and clean together in between making love at every available opportunity. We do our best to keep it from Jacob, which turns out to be easily accomplished—at least at first—since he's oblivious and always running off with Frank in the afternoons. I should be more worried about him disappearing every day, but it's hard to be stressed out when Archer lifts me on top of the dryer in the laundry chalet and shows me how much fun washing sheets and towels can be.

The metal of the machine is warm against my rear, which is good, since Archer tugs my pants down my hips, flinging them somewhere on the floor. He leans back in between my legs, his lips teasing my ear and trailing down my jaw.

I fumble with the zipper on his jeans. "Condom?"

His breath is warm on my neck, his hands clenching around my bare thighs. "Back pocket."

I reach for the packet, rip it open with my teeth, and slide it on.

His mouth finds mine, tongue seeking entrance at the same moment he slides into me with a groan.

Jacob walks in, emits a high-pitched shriek, and then slams the door closed.

Archer drops his head on my shoulder. "I guess we're not keeping secrets anymore."

"Shit." I scramble off the dryer, jerking my pants on while Archer disposes of the condom and zips himself up.

"Jacob." I call his name as I'm leaving the shed. I half expect him to be long gone, to use this as yet another excuse to take off, but he's pacing about twenty feet away from the door.

Archer emerges behind me and stops at my shoulder, close enough to touch if I lean back.

Jacob stops pacing and points at him. "You said you wouldn't sleep with my sister."

"I never said that."

Jacob goes back to his frantic pacing and then throws up his hands. "You said you respected her."

Archer frowns. "You should respect all the women

you sleep with and the ones you don't. What is wrong with you?"

Jacob fists his hair with both hands and tugs. "I don't know. I can't think straight." His eyes fall shut. "I really wish I hadn't seen your ass."

I glance over my shoulder at Archer. He's grinning.

"Are you enjoying this?" I ask in a low voice.

Jacob's face contorts like he's in pain.

"Kind of." Archer shrugs, still smiling. Then he calls out to Jacob, "Would it help if you showed me your ass?"

Jacob pauses his agitated strides, scratching the back of his head, face contorted in confusion. "Maybe? Ugh." He covers his eyes with one hand and waves at us with the other. "Could you not stand so close to each other?"

"I'll let you handle him from here," Archer whispers in my ear before giving my lobe a little nip.

I shiver and turn my head toward him. "Come over for dinner later?"

"I'll finish with the laundry and changing the sheets, and then I'll be there." He drops a quick, hard kiss on my mouth before heading back to the laundry chalet.

I make my way over to Jacob and smack him upside the head. "You have no business commenting on my love life."

He holds up his hands to block any further hits. "Hey! I'm looking out for your interests."

"I changed your diapers."

"And I'll probably be changing yours someday."

I cross my arms over my chest. "I am not that much older than you."

"Fine. Whatever. You could've warned me." His face still scrunched in revulsion, he stubs the toe of his boot into the gravel.

"Why were you coming to the laundry chalet, anyway?" It's not exactly his favorite place.

"I was looking for you. Some guy called the office line about an overdue credit card bill?

I wince. "Yeah. There's some stuff we need to talk about. Come on, let's go inside."

We tromp through the melting snow and into the house. I put the kettle on to make tea.

"Okay. What is it?" Jacob leans back against the counter. "Whatever it is, it can't be worse than what I just witnessed."

I grab mugs from the cupboard and set them down. "Archer has an idea that will allow us to keep the house."

"Really?"

I turn around. "Sort of. We'd have to sell off half the ownership interest to Oliver."

His brows lift. "Half? What does that mean?"

I grab the tea bags and sugar from the cupboard while I explain it, telling Jacob everything about the camp and how we would keep the house and live on the property but potentially help with the camp.

He scowls. "A kids' camp? What would I do?"

I hand him his mug of tea. "Probably the same as you've been. But no getting drunk around the kids."

He takes the cup and ignores the comment. Then he sets it on the counter before crossing his arms over his chest, lips pursed. "Is this what you want?"

"I don't know. It might not even happen. But we don't have any other options. This is the best one. If we can't convince Oliver to accept a deal like this, we might lose everything."

He considers that and nods. "As long as the property stays in the family and we keep the house." He sighs. "Whatever you decide, Fin. I support you."

"You do?"

His lips turn down. "I'm not sure if I support whatever you're doing with Archer."

"Jacob. I'm happy."

"Do you love him?"

Do I? It's too soon, isn't it? I know I feel closer to him than I've ever felt to anyone else I've slept with, but is that love?

I have nothing to compare it to. How do you know?

"I don't know. It's too soon for all that. But he's coming back next week after he closes some business deal in Florida, and I guess we'll just wait and see."

"Is he rich?"

I shrug. "I don't know." Based on what I've observed, he has some wealth. He owns his own business, he's friends with Oliver the billionaire, but Archer is not ostentatious. It's just not his style, maybe since he came from so little. Also, I don't care. If he had nothing, I'd still want to be with him.

"Whatever. Just . . . next time you're *together*, keep it behind a locked door, okay? And not anywhere I might hear or see either of you before or after." He grimaces. "I think I might be traumatized."

I chuckle and mess with his hair, scrubbing it with my knuckles like I did when he was little. "You got it."

I wake up in Archer's arms on Thursday morning to the press of gentle kisses against my eyelids.

"I have to get up." His voice is low and graveled from sleep. His lips stroke faint trails down my face to my neck, then he sucks gently on the sensitive spot beneath my ear.

"I don't want you to go," I mumble, wrapping my arms around his neck to keep him in place.

"I'm coming back."

I nod and hang on to him, keeping my hands on his back while he reaches for a condom. I don't let go for a second, gripping his shoulders as he settles between my legs, wrapping my arms around him and hanging on tight while he moves inside me in leisurely thrusts. It's slow and sweet and feels like goodbye.

After, we stay in bed and hold each other until he has no choice but to get up and get dressed or he'll miss his flight. I'm not opposed to it, but I knew this was coming. Besides, it's only a few days, right? I'll just pretend that I'm the same person I was three weeks ago, before he arrived. I'll pretend his leaving isn't going to leave an Archer-sized hole in the fabric of my life.

I wait in the bed, holding onto the heat and the last moments while he moves around the room, packing up his things.

I squint into the sun as I walk with Archer to his rental car. It shouldn't be sunny. It should be grim and desolate to match my mood. I shouldn't have so much apprehension roiling through my stomach. It's as if once he leaves my sight, I'm going to wake up and the past few weeks will be a dream, something that never happened, something I imagined.

The more time I've spent with him, the more I've learned about him—and his body—the harder it is to contemplate any sort of future without him.

I know he's coming back. He's said he's coming back. But for how long? We haven't discussed how long he intends to stay after Florida, as if we're both scared to think about it too much. I can't ask him to move here. That would be crazy, right?

He shuts the trunk and draws me into his arms. "I'll call you when I land."

I squeeze him tighter. "Call me before then."

"I will. I'll text too. And I'll see you next week."

We kiss, our mouths meeting with a hungry

urgency as if he's going to be gone a month instead of a handful of days.

"You're both disgusting," Jacob calls out as he passes by, his arms loaded with firewood.

We break apart, and Archer gives me one last peck. "See you soon," he whispers before getting in the car and driving away.

The rest of the day drags on and on even though I stay busy. We have a few guests coming and going. I prep one of the cabins, but I'm slow and have no motivation. It's as if all the excitement and light disappeared with Archer.

The next day, Friday, I catch Jacob as he's climbing into the truck around two in the afternoon.

"Where are you going?"

"I'm meeting Frank at Veronica's."

I worry my bottom lip between my teeth. "Okay. Don't forget I need the truck tomorrow morning."

"You've told me three times."

"I know, but sometimes when you're out with Frank, you tend to get drunk and forget everything." My voice comes out more snappish than I intend, which can only be because I'm stressed that I can't count on him and I miss Archer. I'm also worried about Piper, who hasn't returned my texts or calls since we spoke the other day.

"You act like I'm some kind of complete alcoholic. I get my work done. I do what you ask. It's not a problem. Stop treating me like a child."

"Stop acting like one."

He swears and gets into the truck, turning it on. "I'm leaving."

"Fine."

"Fine." He slams the door shut and takes off down the drive, going too fast, probably to piss me off.

It's working.

God, what is it about my siblings that makes me revert to middle school?

I stomp into the house and then make my way to the office, slamming myself down in the seat so hard it squeaks in protest.

I take a few deep breaths and then check my phone.

A text from Archer is waiting.

I miss you. It's too hot down here, and boring. No raccoons or laundry chalets in sight.

I smile, some of my frustration ebbing at the connection.

I miss you too. I can't bring myself to clean up your cabin. Every time I look at it, I get turned on.

• • •

I set my phone down, thinking he won't be able to respond right away because he's supposed to be slammed with meetings all day. Warmth spreads through me when my phone dings only a moment later.

You just made me groan out loud and Nora thinks I'm sick. We can talk about your state of arousal tonight. I can't even think of you right now or I'll have to try and get through this next meeting with a boner.

He sends an eggplant emoji.

I chuckle and send him some kissy emoji's and then put my phone back down.

I wish he was here so I could take care of his little problem but also so I could talk to him about Jacob. But it will all have to wait.

The truck isn't here.

I stand at the side door, hand gripping the knob, gazing at the vacant spot in the driveway. My heart thumps a dull beat in my chest. It's almost seven in the morning, and he's still not home.

Maybe he parked out front, even though he's never done that before, ever, and it wouldn't make sense, since he would have to go through the front office, but you never know.

I stalk around to the front.

Nope. No one. He's not here. I wrap my arms around myself, shivering in the early-morning chill, staring at nothing.

This can't be right. I race back inside.

"Jacob?" I knock at his room, listening intently for any response.

Only silence. There are no snores, no irritated grumbles, no shuffling or movement of any kind.

I push the door open. "Jake?" It's empty. I move to the bed, resting a hand on the rumpled sheets. Cold.

"Dammit."

I left my phone in the kitchen.

Stomping back down the stairs, I lean against the counter and try to call him. It goes straight to voicemail.

I should have called Veronica's or something last night, but I was distracted by Archer's phone call and the subsequent conversation that involved his deep voice in my ear, giving me a preview of exactly how he wants to touch me when he returns. So distracted I didn't even tell him about my argument with Jake. Sure, it was nice to not be stressed out all night, but now I'm paying for it.

I call Frank but get his voicemail.

"Shit."

What now?

I put my phone next to me and rub my temples, trying to soothe the growing ache. What if something happened? The truck might have broken down. But then he would answer his phone or call me, right?

Maybe he crashed. A bomb of dread explodes through me. I squeeze my eyes shut on the thought. I can't think that way. Not yet. Maybe he'll show up in a few minutes, full of apologies, so I can wring his neck.

I take a few deep breaths and get dressed quickly, throwing on my leggings and sweater, swiping on a layer of mascara like normal, just in case, my mind sorting through options of what to do, who to call next if he's not home in the next five minutes.

Once that's done, he's still not home.

I go out to the front porch to wait, sitting in the swing, where Archer and I first kissed, but even those memories aren't doing anything to alleviate my rising apprehension.

I try Veronica. "Hello?" she mumbles.

"I'm so sorry to call so early." I wince. I know she works late hours, but she might have been one of the last people to see Jake. "Did you see Jacob last night? He hasn't come home."

She clears her throat. "Jake? Oh. Right. Him and Frank left kinda early last night, I think. It might have been around eight? I'm not really sure of the exact time, but I remember it was before nine, when the band started up."

"Did they happen to say where they were going?"

She is silent for a few seconds. "No. They just paid and left."

I blow out a breath. "Okay. Thanks. Sorry again about calling so early."

"No worries, honey. Let me know when you hear from him. I'm sure they're just sleeping it off at Frank's. He'll probably show up any minute now."

"Yeah, yeah. You're probably right." I hang up and drop my head back against the seat.

I have to do something. I shouldn't have argued with him before he left. Guilt pounds into me every time I pick up my phone and try Frank again. And again. And again, until he finally answers.

"Frank?"

The phone clicks and the line opens, but no one says anything.

It's not quiet though. There's a bunch of rustling in the background and the sound of deep breathing.

Did he answer the phone and then fall back asleep?

"Frank!" I yell.

"Wha-what?" Frank is a year younger than Jacob. He still lives with his parents and works at one of the ski resorts in the winter and then bums around the rest of the year, doing odd jobs.

"Frank!" I shout again.

There's more rustling, and the breathing gets louder. "What's up?"

"Frank. It's Finley."

More breathing. "Yeah?"

"Where's Jacob?"

"Um. Home?"

"He's not here." Lord, give me patience. "Did he go to your place last night?"

"Uh, yep."

"Well, is he still there?"

Seriously, this is like trying to herd a goldfish.

"Lemme see." There's rustling and grunting on the other end. Seconds drag on like years while he shuffles around. "Jake, you still here?" he calls out. "Ma, is Jake still here?"

More silence, the distant sound of another voice.

"I think he left, man."

"But he was there last night?"

"Yeah. He was here. We got so high." He laughs.

God. I drop my head in to my free hand. Drunk and high. Perfect. Knowing it's probably pointless, but having to ask anyway, I try. "Do you know what time he left?"

"Nah, I've been sleeping."

"When did you last see him?"

"Uh, probably like two or something?"

"Great. Thanks." *For nothing.* I hang up and release a frustrated groan. "Jacob. Where are you?" I ask the empty porch.

Maybe . . . maybe I should call the cops or the nearest hospital. My stomach fills with ice-cold despair. I can try Marco first. He's the local sheriff. I pick up my phone to call the station, but I haven't completed dialing when gravel crunches in the distance. Someone is coming.

I stand on the porch, gaze fixed on the curve of the driveway.

Please let it be Jacob.

My breath catches in my throat.

It's not Jacob.

It's not the familiar, faded-green truck parking in front of the house.

It's a police cruiser. The ground drops from beneath my feet, and my entire body flashes hot and cold.

Twenty

ARCHER

"Not many people work on the weekend, and I know tomorrow is Sunday, but we need to sign off on the rest of the paperwork. That way, on Monday, we can tackle staff interviews, and Tuesday, we can work on reorganization. Can you call someone?"

"Sure." I glance down at my phone. Finley hasn't returned my last text.

Nora rattles off the list of upcoming duties as we step into the elevator.

"Dinner later? Jess wants to see you. There are a few good places near the hotel, so we can drink and stumble home."

I'm still staring at my phone, half listening. "Yeah, that sounds good."

"Everything okay?"

"I don't think Finley's getting my messages."

"Did you try calling?"

I nod. "On our last break, but it went straight to voicemail."

"Maybe her phone is dead or something. Didn't you say she's teaching today?"

"Yeah. You're probably right."

The elevator dings, and a couple of people get off while others get on.

"You like this woman a lot, don't you?" Nora asks as the doors slide shut again.

"I do."

Which is why I can't erase this nagging feeling building in my gut that something is wrong. I'm sure it's because of my own issues. I'm probably overreacting, expecting something awful because I've never felt this close to anyone before. Nora's right. She's in class or driving back from Binghampton and going through a dead zone for cell reception. I'm sure she'll call as soon as she can. But the unease continues to shove at me.

On the ground floor, we push out of the large glass doors and into the muggy heat of downtown Miami. It's eighty degrees in the middle of March.

My phone rings, and I'm so on edge, I answer without even checking who it is.

"Finley?"

"Not quite," a deep, familiar voice answers.

"Hey. Oliver." I glance over at Nora, and she sticks out her tongue, making a face. "I'm surprised it took you this long to break my 'no calling' rule."

"You know how lucky you are that I cater to any of your whims."

"So lucky."

"What's the news?"

We walk down the sidewalk in the direction of Nora's car, weaving through pedestrians and skirting a food cart. "I do have an idea for you, and you will get what you want, which is starting the camp, but there are some caveats, and I'm still working on it."

"Let's hear it."

I hesitate. "Are you sure you don't want to wait until I can present something to you in writing?" It would be best if I could list out the positives for him in plain black and white before he can cut me off.

"I don't need that from you yet. Just spill it, Weston."

"You pay Finley half of what you're offering, and then you split the ownership rights. She'll help manage and run the camp plus oversee any renovations and hiring. You'll cover all those expenses, of course."

There's an extended pause. I pull the phone away. He hasn't hung up yet. That's positive.

"Shared ownership?" He says the words the way he might say "filing taxes" or "dental surgery" or "flaming excrement."

"That's the idea."

The line goes dead. I check again. Yep. This time, he hung up.

"What did he say?"

"He hung up on me. So it went better than I expected."

She clicks the button on her key fob, and the lights flash on her silver Honda. "He hung up on you? How is that good?"

"It's not great, but he's reacted worse, and I eventually got him over to my side."

We get in the car, and while she's peering over her shoulder, waiting to merge into traffic, Oliver calls me back.

"Oliver," I answer.

"Shared ownership?" he says again, as if we didn't just have a few minutes' hiatus from the last call. "Have you lost your mind? How is she going to help manage anything? By running it into the ground again?"

"Hang on there. You don't know the circumstances."

"I don't need the circumstances. I've reviewed the numbers, and they don't lie."

"Yes, you do. She has a lot more to offer than you realize."

"Fine," he clips out. "Convince me. You have thirty seconds."

"Finley is one of the hardest workers I've ever met. She's smart, dependable, and she understands loyalty.

She would do anything for her family and the people she cares about."

"Well, that's great for her and her family, Archer, but it's not enough for me."

My mind trips over possibilities and ideas and then lands on something that just might work. "Finley's a former Olympic-level ice skater." True enough. "We'll build a rink on the property. She's already certified to teach kids and teens; she does it every weekend, group and individual classes. It's a win."

He's silent, and I stare out the front window while Nora navigates us through rush-hour traffic.

"Why would you do this to me?" he says eventually.

"Oliver," I open my mouth to spout off another argument for Finley, but what comes out is, "I love her."

The words shoot into the air and then sink into my skin with the truth of it. They feel right. Solid. Pure.

I love her.

It's too fast, but that doesn't make it any less true.

"What?" he groans. "Not this again."

"What do you mean again? I've never—"

"Not you. I had to compromise on another deal last year with Guy Chapman because of a woman. It's like men become incapable of logical functioning because their dicks take over. Love doesn't exist. There's lust and hormones, and that's it."

"Guy Chapman, the chef?"

"Yes, Guy Chapman, the chef. He and that cupcake woman are all over each other. They asked me to be in their wedding next month." He releases a beleaguered sigh.

I know Guy Chapman peripherally, through Oliver and other business associates.

I also know that Guy has custody of his two young sisters, which means he might enjoy doing something for the camp too.

The idea blossoms, growing in scope.

What if they turn the camp into more than a camp? Into a way to teach real skills to these kids—skills that are both fun and functional and teach them something they can potentially use the rest of their lives? We have sports covered, ice sports, anyway, then maybe culinary . . . we could add other skills and areas of interest. The property is large enough that we could even open a student-run restaurant and teach the kids how to manage money, run a cash register, basic business-operating skills for the older kids. My mind races with the possibilities. We could sell tickets for skating events and hockey games to help with funding.

"I'm not sharing," Oliver says. "Love is irrelevant in business. Come up with a new idea. And don't forget to work Piper's art into it. I want a full show with completely original pieces."

He hangs up again.

I slide my phone into my pocket.

"You love her." Nora's tone is smug.

"Do you think I'm crazy?"

"No." She grins over at me before navigating a left-hand turn. "I knew almost as soon as I met Jess. Sometimes, you meet someone, and things just click."

She parks, and we grab our bags and head into the hotel.

Nora turns to me when we're walking through the lobby. "Want to meet down here in an hour for dinner?"

I pull out my phone and check it for a missed text from Finley for the thousandth time.

Nothing.

"Yeah. Dinner in an hour sounds great."

My phone rings. This time, I look before answering.

It's her. Just seeing her name on the screen lifts my spirits and removes the giant boulder of worry that's been sitting on my chest all day.

"Finley. How are you? How was class?" The staggering relief has left me a little lightheaded, my words emerging in a rush.

"Archer. I'm so sorry I couldn't call you sooner. My phone was dead. The nurse brought me a charger and—"

My heart drops. "Wait. A nurse?"

"Yes." Her voice cracks on the word. "Jacob's in the hospital."

Twenty-One

FINLEY

"I'm on my way."

"You can't—Archer. Don't you have to be there for at least the next week? I can't ask you to—"

"Baby, you're more important than anything else. I'll be on the next flight out." He speaks to someone nearby, talking in a low voice, something about the airport and a car, and I take a full breath for the first time in twelve hours.

The darkness enveloping my vision since the patrol car pulled into the drive lightens just a bit.

He's coming. He'll be here. He'll fix it like he fixed the radiator and got rid of the raccoon. Okay, so maybe he can't fix this as easily as those things, but just listening to his voice gives me hope.

"Her brother is in the hospital." He comes back on the line. "Is he okay? What happened?"

"Car accident. He's going to be okay, they said, but he needed surgery because he broke his femur."

"What hospital are you at?"

"Binghampton General." I swallow past a dry throat. When was the last time I drank some water? I don't even know. "The truck is totaled. The sheriff drove me here, but he left."

"Is there anyone with you?"

I glance around the half-full waiting room. I'm sitting by myself in a corner, close to the outlet where I've plugged in my phone. "Not yet. Mindy should be here soon. She left the city a few hours ago."

"What do you need? Is there anything that needs to be taken care of at the cottages?"

I try to think. "No. I called in one of our high school volunteers before I called you."

"Nora is already searching for a flight. I'll be there as soon as I can, okay?"

My hand grips the phone as if I can reach through it and hang on to him and have him hold me and tell me everything is going to be okay.

"Finley, I—I'll see you soon."

"Okay."

I hang up the phone, and once the connection is severed, I immediately want to cry. He's coming. But it's not likely he'll get a flight out tonight. It's after five. I won't see him until tomorrow morning, if I'm lucky.

I should call someone—Veronica, Reed, someone who can go over to the cottages and make sure everything is okay—I think we had some guests checking in today—but I can't think of anything right now. All my motivation is zapped. I stare at my phone and slump down further on the padded plastic seat.

Jake was driving early in the morning. He hit an icy spot and spun out into a tree. He was going too fast. He was wearing his seat belt, but it's an old truck with no airbag. The windshield shattered.

In addition to the broken leg, he might have a concussion or some kind of brain injury. Not to mention all of the bumps and bruises and scratches and I don't even know what else. They did a test, and his blood alcohol level was over the legal limit, and he had traces of cannabis.

Marco said he thinks maybe Jake tried to sleep it off, but clearly, he didn't sleep long enough. He was probably worried I would be mad if he was late or something. Remorse pounds at me for fighting with him yesterday.

Thankfully, Marco is going to suggest they waive jail time if Jacob goes to rehab and does community service, since it's his first offense and no one else was hurt. There was no property damage other than our truck and the tree. He came to the house as a courtesy, because we've known him our whole lives, and he knew I would need a ride to the hospital. One of the only benefits to small-town living.

I haven't been able to reach Piper. She's not answering her phone or responding to texts. I didn't tell her what was going on; I just texted for her to call me when she has a chance. It doesn't seem like something I should spill out over a text message.

"Finley." A familiar voice calls my name.

"Mindy." She's speed walking across the waiting room. I stand up to greet her, and she wraps me in a hug, smelling like high-priced perfume and home. Her dark-blue blazer is soft under my fingers.

She's always so put together. By comparison, I am a slob, dressed in leggings and an oversized sweater, my hair pulled back in a messy bun. At least I still have mascara on. I've been too shocked to cry.

I lean back, still holding her arms. "Your hair. You changed it."

She has dark hair like me and Taylor. Now it's been highlighted and cut in a sleek bob that frames her face.

She fingers a strand. "I did. But tell me about Jacob. How is he? Any updates?"

"He's going to be okay. They're doing surgery on his leg because it was broken in the crash."

She winces and rubs my arm. "Have you heard from the others?"

I sit back down in my chair. "Taylor is on her way from Tennessee. It's a fourteen-hour drive, so I think she'll be here by tomorrow, midday. I haven't been able to reach Piper to explain things, and I didn't want to leave it on a voicemail or tell her via text."

She sits next to me. "I can try too. We can tag team her. She'll have to realize something's going on then." She pulls her phone and laptop out of her briefcase.

"Sorry." She gives me an apologetic look when my gaze lands on her computer. "I shouldn't have brought it, but I need something else to focus on."

"I understand." I'm the same way. Throwing myself into rescuing the struggling family business, working until I can hardly think, stand, or feel. Going and going and going until I'm numb.

And this is the result of that. Right? I've spent every day of my life since Aria died working, thinking perhaps if I worked harder, if I fixed the mess at the cottages, it would somehow fix everything else. If I saved the property, I could save everyone, and all the problems would go away. But they've only gotten worse.

By working so hard, obsessively attempting to wrangle control of something, I've lost control of everything.

But I *can't* control everything. No one can.

Jacob has to want to change and put in the work to make it so. Piper has to want to leave; she has to get out herself or ask for my help. But I can't make her. Nothing I do or say will change their minds.

And nothing I do will bring Aria back. That's the crux of it, isn't it? I can't control the fact that I wasn't there when my baby sister needed me most. I wasn't there to watch out for her. I can't go back and change the past.

Which means letting go of the things I've been holding on to so hard. They're not supports; they're weights, tying me down.

"Finley?"

I turn toward Mindy. "What?"

"I asked you a question twice, and you were totally zoned out. Are you sure you're okay?"

"Yeah. I'm fine. Sorry. Just . . . thinking. It's been a long day."

She clucks in sympathy. "I booked a hotel room less than a mile away if you want to go shower, take a nap, or something?"

I shake my head. "I can't sleep. I'm not going anywhere until we hear more from the doctor. What were you asking?"

"Why didn't you tell me Jacob's drinking had gotten this bad?"

I bite my lip. "I didn't want to worry you."

"Finley." She reaches over, putting a hand on my arm. "You can't do everything alone. Let me help you."

"I don't want to—"

"Finley." She sits up, removing her hand from my arm and glaring at me. "Next time you need anything, promise you'll let me help, or I will tell everyone about your childhood obsession with that Teenage Mutant Ninja Turtle body pillow."

I groan and cover my face, laughing behind my

hands. "Fine. I promise. But honestly, it's been better. Archer's been a big help, actually."

Her brows lift. "Archer. The guy from the other morning." She leans back in her seat, tapping a finger on her chin. "What is happening with that?"

Thinking about Archer jolts something in my chest. "We're together, I guess." My face heats. It sounds so . . . immature. We haven't had that whole exclusivity conversation, not really. In the past week, we've spent more time naked than conversing. But it feels serious, and it can't be one-sided.

Mindy's brows lift. "Together, huh? That happened quick."

"I guess so. But everything is different with Archer. It's hard to describe." How could I explain to anyone the connection, the caring, and how it is between us?

"Can't imagine it." She shakes her head.

"Maybe if you took some time off, a vacation, or learned to relax a little, then you could find a hunk too."

She snorts. "Like you did?"

"You're right. He basically fell into my lap. Shoved there by Oliver Nichols of all people."

Our conversation is cut short when Jacob's doctor emerges from behind a set of double doors in the corner. I immediately stand up and move toward her, Mindy hot on my heels.

"He's okay. Surgery went well. Luckily, it was a transverse fracture, and there was no damage to the supporting ligaments. He also has a moderate brain injury, and we had to drain some fluid around his brain. We'll continue to monitor the swelling."

Mindy squeezes my hand.

The doctor continues. "He's sleeping now, but once the meds wear off, you can see him, although he may still be out of it. He has some bruising and scratches on his face and a lot of monitoring devices, so he looks worse for the wear, but it's not as bad as it seems. With enough rest and a little bit of time, he should make a full recovery."

"Thank you so much, Doctor," I say.

She gives a short nod. "Someone will be out to get you as soon as he's ready."

As soon as she disappears behind the doors, Mindy and I collapse against each other, hugging in relief.

The doctor warned us that Jacob would look bad, but I can't stop the gasp that escapes when we walk into his recovery room.

His face is swollen, bruised, and scraped. He has lacerations up and down his arms. His leg is up in a sling and in a cast to the hip.

It's like every nightmare, every worry and anxiety I've had since Aria died has been laid out in front of me in physical form.

"Jesus," Mindy says. "At least he's sleeping."

A nurse is in the room, checking his IV. "We'll monitor him closely for a couple of hours while the anesthesia wears off," he says. "Then he'll be taken to an inpatient room, where you can spend more time with him."

"Thank you," Mindy tells him before he leaves the room to give us a few minutes.

My eyes are locked on Jake's still form. His chest moves up and down with his slow breathing. Has this been his death wish all along? He has lived recklessly ever since Aria died. Is this close enough? Will this be enough to shake him from the stupor? Or is he going to have to keep going until he joins her on the other side?

My chest aches at the thoughts, my eyes watering, but I don't cry. I can't cry, not yet. I have to stay strong.

Mindy rests a careful hand over his. "Oh, Jake." Her voice is just above a whisper. "I'm sorry I haven't been here." She looks over at me. "I'm so sorry, Fin. I didn't know things were so bad."

I shake my head. "There's nothing you could have done."

She steps toward me, putting an arm around my shoulders. "You okay?"

My back teeth clench. I swallow past a lump in my throat. I'm not okay. But I have to be.

"I'm fine." We stand together next to his bed, the steady beat of the monitors the only sound.

He's going to get through this, the doctor said. He'll make a full recovery. I grasp that thin thread of hope like it's the only thing keeping me from having a full-blown meltdown.

A few minutes later, the nurse takes us back out to the waiting room, letting us know they'll tell us once they move Jacob to his inpatient room.

I take deep breaths, trying to hold it together, hanging onto the knowledge that he's going to be all right. After he recovers and has physical therapy, he will be okay. It's like a mantra I have to keep repeating to myself. Seeing him in that bed, bruised and broken, brings all the emotions rushing back from when Aria died. Guilt. Anger. Sadness. But at least this time, it's not total despair.

He's going to be okay.

I need a break.

"Can I take you up on that hotel room shower offer?"

She rubs my arm. "Of course." Digging into her briefcase, she hands me the keys to her car, the confirmation number for the hotel reservation, and her wallet so I can check in for her, since she came straight to the hospital.

"I have a bag of clothes in the trunk," she adds.

Thankfully, we are similar in size, except she's a few inches taller, so I can borrow something to change into.

Of course, she's staying at the nicest place in the immediate area, the kind with plush white robes, designer shampoo, and shiny marble floors in the lobby.

After I've showered, Mindy texts and asks me to bring back some dinner, so I grab some takeout for both of us on my way back.

I'm walking down the hallway toward the waiting room, food bags in hand, when I spot him, talking to Mindy.

My heart flips in my chest. I didn't think he would be here until tomorrow at the earliest.

I'm a human statue in the middle of the hospital corridor. I drink him in. He's wearing dark slacks and a button-up gray long-sleeved shirt. I've never seen him so dressed up, but his jawline is as scruffy as ever. Mindy's nodding at something he's saying, but then she sees me and smiles.

He catches the angle of her gaze, and his head turns in my direction.

Then he's coming toward me, moving in space-eating strides, as quickly as I'm rushing toward him.

The takeout bags drop to the floor when we reach each other, and then his arms are around me. I hang on, relishing the feel of his warmth, his comfort, the way he rubs my back and murmurs in my ear.

Everything I've been holding back since the cop car pulled into the driveway, Jacob in the hospital bed, my guilt over arguing with him, worrying about the aftermath of all of this . . . I haven't cried yet, not even when Mindy got here. But Archer's mere presence knocks down the dam, a hurricane of pent-up chaos I've been keeping shuttered and locked inside. I can let go now.

He's here to hold me together even when I'm falling apart. He's my safe space.

When I finally pull back to wipe my face on something other than his shirt, I'm full of remorse. "I'm so sorry about all of this." I sniff and wipe at my cheeks with the back of my hand. "You missed out on your work and came all this way just for me to get snot all over you. I'm a mess."

He smiles down at me, tucking some hair back behind my ear. "Life is messy sometimes. Whatever happens, we clean it up together."

The words are enough to send a flood of emotion into my eyes again, and I hide my face against his chest. The shirt is already ruined, so I can't make it worse.

How did he become so integral so soon?

How did he become someone who has my back no matter what? Someone who's seen all my dark bits and accepted them? I know with every piece of my soul that I would do anything for him too.

This should be terrifying. I should run for the hills, but I could no sooner remove my heart from my body.

He's the calm in my storm.

Jesus.

I love him.

Twenty-Two

FINLEY

We eat in the waiting room, the three of us. I share my dinner with Archer. Shortly after we finish, a nurse comes out to let us know Jacob is settled in his room.

Even though I know the extent of his injuries, seeing him again is still a shock.

Archer grasps my hand in silent support.

"Hey, Jacob." Mindy reaches his bedside first.

His eyes follow her, still a little glassy from the meds. When Archer and I move next to her at his bedside, his gaze flickers to us.

He tries to speak but manages only a croak.

"It's okay," I tell him. "We'll talk later. We just wanted you to know we're here. We'll be here in the morning when you wake up too."

I rest my fingers over his, not wanting to touch him too hard. Even his hand is bruised.

He blinks a few times, and then his eyes droop and fall shut.

Archer puts his arm around my shoulders.

Mindy links her elbow through mine on my other side.

The doctor comes in, going over some of what to expect before we leave.

"He's going to be in the hospital for at least a week, then he'll need physical therapy," she tells us.

She keeps talking, but my mind is going over everything. Once he's physically able, he's likely going to end up in a rehab facility to satisfy the court require-ments—depending on what the judge decides when that gets sorted.

It's a lot to take in, but the bottom line is that he will be okay. Eventually.

God, I hope so.

We head over to the hotel. Archer gets us a room a couple floors down from Mindy, and after saying goodnight and promising to meet in the lobby the next morning, we split into our respective rooms.

As soon as the door shuts, I get rid of my shoes and flop back on the bed. Archer joins me, and like two magnets, we immediately flip toward each other. We lie on our sides, still fully clothed, my leg over his hip and his arm under my head.

"I'm a little worried about when Taylor gets here." I

release a deep breath and relax further when Archer trails a hand through my hair.

"Why?"

"She and Mindy don't get along. They've been in some weird fight for a year."

The pads of his fingers rub into my scalp, and I shut my eyes on a groan. "I'll give you an hour to stop doing that."

He chuckles and continues to massage my head for a minute before asking, "Do you know what they're fighting about?"

"No. They won't tell me."

"Sounds like something they need to work out between themselves."

I frown. "What if they don't?"

He kisses the corner of my mouth, effectively removing the sulk. "I don't know. But you're family, right? You and Jake argue too, but you still love each other. They're both coming here and will be here for Jacob despite whatever's happening with them. As long as you all still have each other, what's the worst that could happen?"

"You're right." I blow out a breath and open my eyes. "I was thinking earlier about how I keep trying to control everything, but I can't control my sisters or Jacob, and yet here I am, trying to control them again."

"You worry because you care, and that's a good thing. You also raised them. It's only natural to feel like a surrogate mother. You may not be able to control Taylor and Mindy, but you can love them."

"I can. I do." I take in his face, his strong jaw, kissable lips, kind eyes. I want to tell him I love him too. The words are ready to burst out of me, but it's too soon. I know he cares about me. I know he feels strongly about me. He wouldn't be here otherwise. But I'm too unsure, too insecure. What if he doesn't say it back right away? What if he needs more time?

I blink at him, shaking my head slowly. "How do you do it?"

"Do what?"

"Make me feel better just by being here? Thank you for listening."

He kisses my nose. "You've been doing so much by yourself for so long. It's okay to need a little bit of understanding."

I brush my lips against his. "A little?" I laugh. "I need a truckload, and somehow, you provide it. How did you get here so quickly, anyway? I wasn't expecting you until at least tomorrow."

His responding smile is a tad sheepish. "I might have bribed someone and then also bought them a first-class-to-anywhere-international ticket in order to get onto the next available flight."

My brows lift. "You bribed someone and then, on top of that, bought them a first-class ticket to anywhere they wanted? Wasn't that expensive?"

He shrugs. "I can afford it."

I push up a little, resting my head on my hand. "I figured you had some money, but I didn't know it was that kind of money."

He chuckles at my vexed tone. "Does it matter?"

I open my mouth to respond in the affirmative and then stop. Does it? I wouldn't ask him for anything like that, and it doesn't really matter to me. I bite my lip. "No. I guess not." I snuggle back down and press closer to him.

His length—which has been gently prodding me this entire time—expands further under my thigh, growing rigid.

I chuckle. "Someone's happy to see me."

"Ignore him. He doesn't understand he's being inappropriate right now. This is snuggle time, not sexy time."

"I think he wants something from me."

"Pretty sure he always wants something from you. But he doesn't get a say."

I lift a brow. "Do I get a say?"

A slow smile spreads across his face. "You get all the says. You get every say."

I sigh, tracing a finger across his prickled jaw and down his neck to the first button on his shirt. "I really missed you."

"I missed you more." And then he tugs me underneath him, clothes become unnecessary, and he shows me just how much more.

The next morning, we're all hanging around in Jacob's room. He's sleeping; Mindy is in a chair in the corner, working on her laptop; Archer and I are sitting closer to Jacob's bed, talking quietly. A soap opera plays on the TV hanging in the corner, the volume too low for us to decipher most of the dialogue.

Taylor rushes into the room. "Oh, my God." She rushes to Jacob's side, blinking away tears. "I can't believe this! You said he looked bad, but I, I didn't—"

"I know. He's going to be okay." I move over to her, wrapping an arm around her shoulder.

"Here come the waterworks." Mindy closes her laptop and sets it on the table next to her.

Taylor twists out of my arms. "Hi, Mindy. It's nice to see you too."

Mindy stands. "I'm going to get coffee. Anyone want one?"

"No, thank you," Archer says.

"I'm good," I say.

"I would love one," Taylor says, her voice brimming with faux sweetness.

Without another word, Mindy stalks out of the room.

Taylor takes a deep breath and blows it out. "She's impossible." But then her eyes widen, and she looks back and forth between us, her mouth dropping open.

"I knew it! How long have you two been a thing, you sly dogs?"

We exchange a glance.

"Not long," I say.

Archer changes the subject. "How was the drive?" he asks Taylor.

Fortunately, it's enough to distract her, for now anyway. She shoots me a speaking look that tells me we will be talking later when Archer isn't around, but for now, we chat about her trip, the weather, nothing at all, and then I give her more of the details about Jacob's prognosis.

Once she's been brought up to speed, Taylor asks if she can use our hotel room to shower, and Archer gives her the spare keycard.

Only a few minutes later, Mindy returns, standing in the doorway and staring at us with her lips pressed into a thin line.

"What is it?" I ask.

"Where is Taylor?"

"She went to the hotel to grab a shower," Archer explains.

She blows out an annoyed breath. "Typical." She sets one of the cups on the table next to Jake and takes a sip from the one in her hand.

"What do you mean?" I know they've been fighting, but there is genuine hostility in Mindy's tone.

"She asks me to get her coffee, which I do because I'm a nice person, then she completely forgets and leaves before I get back. She's always thinking about herself and never considering anything else. Let me guess: she went to your room. Heaven forbid she should rent her own." Her eyes roll upward in annoyance.

I attempt diplomacy. "Well, she doesn't need to rent a room. She has her van."

A bark of laughter escapes her. "Right, the perfect excuse to use everybody else's amenities."

"It's not a big deal. It's not as if it's costing me anything for her to use the shower." Irritation brushes a hand up my spine. Why can't everyone just get along?

"She needs to get a real job and stop running around like she's still in high school. She needs to grow up." She puts her coffee cup down, crossing her arms over her chest.

"Mindy." I move to her side, taking her hand in mine. If there's one thing I can understand, it's being forced to be responsible when everyone around you is enjoying the fruits of their misspent youth. I never had the opportunity, and neither did Mindy. We were thrust into our roles as the eldest siblings too young, too early. "I won't get involved in whatever is going on between the two of you, but we aren't here for you to battle it out. We are here for Jake, and you need to let it go for him. The antagonizing needs to stop. For Jake and for me. Please."

She sighs. "Fine. You're right. It's only hospital

coffee. I drop more change in the homeless guy's bucket every time I pass." She gives me a wry smile. "I'll just think of her as a charity case. I'll do my best to keep my opinion to myself."

"That's fair."

Jacob shifts in the bed, his hand lifting toward the cup of water at his bedside. Mindy grabs it, bringing the straw to his lips since his movements are still limited.

I walk over to Archer's side. He squeezes my hand in silent support.

I love how he lets me fight my own battles, offering his support but not interfering.

My blood pressure drops a few notches. I have enough to worry about with Jacob and the conversation I have to have with him—something I want to do without the others present and when he's in a better state. I don't need to add their troubles to my list of things to stress over. At least this way, I can try and get through the next few days with Jacob—after they return to their regular lives—without listening to incessant bickering.

The nurse comes in to check Jacob's blood pressure and give him some pain meds and anti-inflammatories.

Before the meds kick in, Jacob is a little more alert.

"You were in a car accident. Do you remember any of it?" I ask.

"Not really." His voice is rough.

I relay to him what we know: how he hit the tree and the things the doctor said about his recovery times.

He nods, wincing slightly and gesturing for more water.

Mindy holds the cup, helping him get the straw into his mouth. "Are you sure this wasn't all part of a grand plan to have us all waiting on you hand and foot?"

He swallows the water, and a corner of his mouth twitches. "I might have tried for something less painful."

He manages a few more drinks of water, but not much time passes before he's asleep again.

Taylor returns, her phone pressed to her ear. "I got Piper on the phone." She moves to my side, putting the phone on speaker.

"Hey, Piper. We've been trying to reach you," I say.

"I'm so sorry." Her voice is low and quavering. "Taylor told me what's going on. I wish I could be there."

"You can be here. It's not like you can't afford a plane ticket," Mindy says.

"Leave her alone," Taylor murmurs.

Mindy shoots her a glare. "She can stand up for herself."

I groan. "Sorry, Piper. As you can see, you aren't missing a whole lot."

Mindy winces, tossing me an apologetic glance.

A deep voice rumbles in the background. "Who are you talking to?"

Ben.

"Hold on a sec," Piper says. "My little brother was in an accident. I need to go home." Her voice is muffled as if she's covered the receiver with her hand, but her words are still audible.

Ben's response is hazier. The tightness in the pitch of his voice is the only thing that's apparent from this side of the line. He speaks for a while, a minute or more, and I strain to make out the words.

Once he's finished, Piper's response is a low, "Okay." She comes back on the phone, the volume clearer but the tone laced in strain. "I can't come now. It's not a good time."

The sick feeling in my gut is mirrored on the stricken faces of Taylor and Mindy in front of me.

I guess this is one thing we can all agree on.

I lean closer to the phone, lowering my voice. "Piper, do you need a rutabaga?"

We wait in heavy silence for her response.

"I have to go."

The line goes dead.

"Well, fuck." Mindy blows out a breath.

"My thoughts exactly." Taylor shakes her head, then she frowns at me. "What's up with rutabaga?"

CHAPTER
Twenty~Three

I had intended to talk to Jacob about the consequences of his crash by myself, but my sisters won't hear of it.

"You promised you'd let me help," Mindy tells me when we step into the hall to talk.

"You have to work tomorrow morning," I remind her.

"So? I can stay until nine or ten at the very least. I can survive on a few hours of sleep. It's not a big deal."

"She's right," Taylor says. "This is a conversation you shouldn't have alone."

I blow out a breath. They're not going to budge. The identical set of their jaws is familiar, and stubbornness is a family trait. I know when I'm outnumbered.

"Fine. We'll have to time it before they give him meds again so he's somewhat alert."

Mindy nods. "Let's talk to the nurses."

They tell us they're going to give him his next round after dinner, so we have a little time to prepare.

Before Archer leaves to grab food for everyone, he gives me a quick kiss and a whispered, "Good luck."

It's time for a genuine conversation with Jacob.

My palms sweat, my heart thudding a dull beat in my chest. I should have talked to him about his drinking sooner. Maybe this wouldn't have happened . . . or maybe it would have happened sooner. It doesn't matter now, and I can't avoid the conflict any longer.

At least Mindy and Taylor are here. Despite my protestations, their combined presence is a soothing balm on what will likely be a tense conversation.

I sit in the chair next to his bedside. "I know you've been through a lot and you're still in pain, but we need to talk about what's going to happen next."

His head tilts toward me. "You mean the physical therapy? You told me about that."

Mindy perches on the arm of my seat. "We mean after that. You had alcohol in your blood, Jacob, over the legal limit."

He blinks. "I tried to sleep it off before I drove home."

I try to keep my voice soft and even. "Not enough. Marco said since it's a first offense, he's going to push for no jail time, and they're going to recommend you pay a fine in addition to completing treatment at an inpatient center for three months." A typical low-grade DUI that doesn't involve other parties doesn't normally incur in-house rehab, but Marco and the rest of the town are more than aware of Jacob's troubles. This offer is a ladder out, a way to hopefully avoid future—potentially worse—damages.

His head rolls away from us, toward the window.

"This might be a good thing," Taylor says.

He squeezes his eyes shut. "How is it a good thing?"

I take a deep breath. "It's a good thing because we love you, Jacob, and things need to change."

"Why are you all ganging up on me?" His eyes open, glaring at the three of us in turn.

"We're not ganging up on you. We want to help." Taylor puts her hand on his arm.

He tugs away from her touch. "I don't need help. But I guess I don't have a say in that."

The bitterness in his voice knocks me back on my heels.

Mindy speaks. "You had a choice, Jacob. You chose to drink and drive. You created this situation. Not us. Not the police. You."

He turns his head away again. "You don't understand."

"I want to understand. Explain it to me."

He swallows before speaking. "You all lost a little sister. I lost a piece of my soul."

Aria.

He never talks about her. We never talk about her.

My eyes fill with tears.

Mindy stares at him, her mouth half open. Taylor's face is stricken, her eyes shiny.

"It was my fault." His voice is dull.

"What?" Taylor asks. "What do you mean? You lost control because of the ice."

"No. Not that. Before."

I shake my head in denial. He can't be talking about Aria still, right?

"It was an accident." I reach for his hand, trying to hold it, trying to get through to him, but his fingers don't grip mine. It's like he can't even feel me.

His head moves back and forth. "It doesn't matter. I'll always be broken. Drinking just helps me forget that a part of me is gone forever."

I exchange bewildered glances with my sisters.

He keeps his eyes squeezed shut and his lips pressed together, his breathing erratic.

We sit in silence. Tears track down my face.

I knew he was struggling. I knew he needed help. But I didn't comprehend, not really. How could I? I was too focused on my own problems, my own issues, my own grief, the business . . . everything.

Eventually, it's clear he's fallen asleep, his breathing slow and steady.

"What do we do now?" Taylor asks in a low voice.

"I don't know." I wish I did.

CHAPTER
Twenty-Four

Archer

Finley's worried eyes meet mine. "Maybe we should wait longer before we give him all this. What if he needs more time? He's barely speaking. He probably won't listen or care anyway."

I lift Finley's hand to my lips, brushing a kiss against her fingers before returning our hands to my lap and tightening my free hand on the steering wheel, driving us into the hospital parking lot.

Since Taylor is here, but only for another day or two to help with the cottages, we were able to escape to visit Jacob and give him some information on the inpatient rehab we found.

"It's time, and it's the right thing to do. I think he

cares. Or he will, eventually. We have to give him the knowledge and then give him the time."

She nods and turns to look out the window. She doesn't have to tell me what she's thinking—we've talked about Jacob a lot over the past few days since she told him about rehab.

I think it might be a good sign, but Finley is struggling, understandably, and she feels like she's sucked me into her family drama, no matter how I try to reassure her. I always wanted a family, and now I have one. Even a broken one is better than nothing, but that's the crux of it. I don't think Jacob is broken, or Mindy and Taylor. Bruised and battered, perhaps. They have strong hearts, and they love each other. Anything can be built—or rebuilt—on a solid foundation.

Until Jacob deals with his guilt over Aria's death, though, I'm not sure what anyone can do to help.

We run into one of Jacob's nurses on our way to his room.

"Oh, good, you brought him some food?" Her whole face brightens. "We haven't been able to get him to eat much."

Finley turns her worried eyes to me, and I take her hand before we enter Jacob's room.

"Jacob. We brought you some ribs from Veronica's. Your favorite."

He doesn't say anything. He's pale and listless and focused on the TV.

"Okay. I'll put them over here." She sets them on a table within reach.

She meets my eyes and then nods toward the TV, and I pick up the remote from the tray table next to Jacob and turn it off.

"We wanted to talk to you." Finley stops at his bedside.

His eyes move from the blank TV screen over to Finley.

I guess that's something.

She takes a breath. "They said you can be released to home next week. We'll set you up downstairs. Steps will be too tricky with your cast. You should be able to get it off in four to six months. After going through physical rehab, you'll go to stay at the inpatient facility." She pulls the pamphlet from her purse. "We brought you some information. We found a nice place. We've called and spoken with the director and some of the staff, and they plan on working with you for grief therapy in addition to the alcohol treatment."

He doesn't say anything, doesn't even acknowledge that she's speaking.

I give her an encouraging smile, and she continues.

"It's like a resort, really. They have a gym and a pool, lots of different forms of entertainment, and a whole staff to cook and clean."

It is the best place we could find. I offered to foot the bill, but Mindy had already covered it.

When Finley finishes speaking, he doesn't say anything or respond in any way, his face a blank mask. Silence fills the space like an invisible, poisonous gas.

Part of me wants to shake Jacob until he sees reason, but it won't help. He's hurting Finley. Can't he see that? Doesn't he know how much love he still has in his life?

"You've got it all figured out, I guess," he says finally.

Her jaw tightens. "You still have a say in some things."

"Do I?" His tone is belligerent.

"We all have to deal with the consequences of our actions. So you'll deal, and then things will get better."

He stares at her for a second and then rolls his head away toward the window. "It's fine, Finley. I'm tired now." His voice is dull, lifeless.

"Okay, Jakey." She squeezes his shoulder. "We'll see you tomorrow."

Her eyes are shiny. She leaves the room.

I stand to follow Finley out but only make it one step before I turn around. I wasn't going to get involved, but I have to say something. "If I had even one person in my life who loved me as much as Finley loves you, I would fight like hell to keep it. I know you've been suffering for a long time, and I can't pretend I could even fathom the losses you've been dealt. But grief is the price we pay for love. Given the choice between grief and nothing, I'd choose grief. Every time. You would too, even though you can't see it yet."

"Can I ask you a question?" Finley lets go of the hand sander and sits back on her heels.

"You can ask me anything."

We're fixing the hardwood in what we now call the raccoon cabin. Finley has been sanding down some of the deeper scratches left behind on the floor by our furry friend, while I've been working on cleaning up the smaller scratches.

Taylor left a couple hours ago, and now it's only the two of us. There are no guests in residence; Finley had to block out reservations over the next few days because of everything going on, and Taylor couldn't stay. Her high school volunteers have school and other obligations during the week, so it was the best choice.

"When do you have to leave again?" Her gaze is steady on mine.

I put down the cloth I've been using and wipe my hands on my jeans. "I'm not really sure. Are you sick of me already?"

She rubs her lips together. "No. If I'm being honest, I'm scared you're going to leave someday soon, and I won't have any warning."

"Finley. I'm not planning on going anywhere any time soon. Unless you want me to?"

"Of course not. But I know you have a job. You have work that you need to travel for, and I don't want to take you from your life because of my family drama."

I crawl toward her. When I get close enough that our knees are touching, I cup one side of her face in my palm, tilting her head toward me. "I travel so much because I haven't had a home in over a decade. Not a real home. Before you came into my life, I was . . . I was lonely."

Her mouth opens, her eyes widening.

I speak again before I lose my nerve.

"I don't have to travel like I was. I never had to. I just didn't have anywhere else to go. I'll have to go out of town for a few days here and there, but there's a lot I can do remotely. Plus I have Nora, and if you were to have fewer obligations around here, you could come with me sometimes when I have to leave."

She stares at me, stricken.

My heart stops beating. "Is it too soon for this conversation?" My head drops, and I let go of her, pulling away. "It's weird, isn't it? Did I make it weird? Forget I sa—"

She reaches for me, using a finger to lift my head up before pressing her soft mouth to mine. "It's not too fast. I don't want you to leave," she whispers against my lips. "Stay." She kisses me again. "Stay." Her hands smooth up my chest, grabbing the collar of my shirt to pull me closer. "Stay."

She unbuttons my shirt, pushes it off my shoulders, and runs greedy hands over my chest. Her mouth follows her hands.

My breathing picks up, every cell in my body coming alive under her fingers.

Her phone buzzes and chimes, vibrating on the floor a few feet away.

She groans in frustration and fumbles for it. "It might be Jacob." She pauses, her gaze on the screen. "I don't recognize the number." Her troubled eyes lift to mine. "It's an LA area code." She accepts the call. "Hello?" Her hand reaches for me, grabbing my leg. "Piper? Hey, what's—? What? Hold on, honey. Slow down. I can't understand you. Why are you using someone else's phone?"

She pulls the phone from her ear and puts it on speaker.

"—but I couldn't bring anything with me." Piper's voice is high and thin with nerves. "I don't have my phone. I don't have my purse. I don't have any ID or anything. I was lucky to get out of there with the clothes on my back. I had to borrow this nice lady's cell phone, but I don't know what to do now. I have nowhere to go. I can't go back there, Finley." She breaks down into messy, noisy tears.

"What diner are you at?" Finley asks.

I'm already reaching for my phone to call Mason. He's in LA somewhere.

"I'm at Teddy's Café."

Finley stares at me. "Who are you calling?"

"I have a friend who owes me a favor."

Twenty~Five

Finley

"I have a friend in LA." He speaks louder for Piper. "He can get you somewhere safe while we work on the next steps, okay?" He puts his phone to his ear.

"Finley, who is that?" Piper's voice escalates in volume.

"It's Archer, he's my . . . he's my . . . he's . . .mine."

His smile is brilliant but quick. "Mason? It's Archer. Hey, man, listen, I'm calling in a favor. How close are you right now to Teddy's Café?"

While they're talking, I ask Piper, "What happened?"

She sniffs. "I wanted to come, to see Jacob. We fought."

We. She means Ben. The asshat.

"I told him I had to leave. Not for like, ever, just to visit for a day or two. But he wouldn't let me. I was going to come anyway, so before he left for work, he took my purse, my phone, and then he"—she swallows and takes a couple of quick breaths—"he locked me in the bathroom."

"What?" Blind rage turns my vision red.

Archer lifts his brows at the anger and incredulity in my tone.

"Maybe I should go back," Piper says.

"What?" I almost drop the phone in shock. "Go back?"

"He's going to be so upset when he realizes I left. It will just make things worse. Maybe I'm crazy, but you don't know him. He needs me."

I have to keep calm for Piper's sake, but it's a losing battle.

"You're not crazy. He's making you think his behavior is normal when he's actually a piece of shit, and I'm going to murder him with my bare hands." Sort of calm, at least.

"I-I know you're right. I want to come home, Fin."

"I'm working on it."

Archer moves the phone away from his mouth. I nod at him.

"What is she wearing?"

"Why is he asking that?" Piper's voice wobbles.

"Mason is on his way," Archer calls out. "He's

going to get you somewhere safe. I want to make sure he can find you."

"Mason is Archer's friend?" she asks.

"Yes. You can trust him, I promise."

She hesitates. "Okay. I'm wearing black joggers and a pink sweater."

Archer relays the information to Mason. Then he speaks louder for Piper's benefit. "Mason will be there in thirty minutes. He's about six foot three, two hundred pounds, dark hair, and he's wearing—" he breaks off. "Seriously?" he chuckles. "He's wearing a sparkly shirt with a unicorn-poop emoji on it." Pause. "And jeans."

I speak into the phone. "Stay where you are and get something to eat or drink."

"I don't have any money."

"I'll call the diner right now and give them my card info, okay?"

"Okay, Finley. I have to give this woman back her phone. But all my things, all my art, everything is still at home."

Archer speaks before I can. "We're going to figure it out. Finley and I are going to find a way to get your things and get you home."

I stare at him in surprise. He speaks into the phone. "Take her somewhere nice. I'll send you the money. Text me the address and let me know when she's checked in."

"We'll see you as soon as we can, okay?" I say to Piper.

I hang up with her, and Archer hangs up with Mason.

We stare at each other, still sitting on the floor on our knees. I shake my head at him and groan. "My life is a mess. Why did you pick me?"

He leans over and kisses me, a gentle brush of his lips over mine. "I knew you were the one when Jacob puked on your shoes and you laughed."

A startled chuckle escapes me.

He hauls me into his arms. "We should go there."

"You don't think we should get her a ticket home? That would be easier."

"She doesn't have ID."

"Oh. Right."

"She needs to get all her things, as much as she can. I don't want her trying it on her own. Mason could help, but I'd prefer he have backup since I don't know this Ben character."

I nod. I guess that makes sense. "We can't leave now though, can we? What about Jacob?"

"Quick trip, there and back. Long enough to get Piper and her essentials. We can have stuff shipped later if she needs it."

I drop a quick kiss on his lips. "Let's search for flights."

We leave all the sanding and staining supplies on

the floor, since we can clean it up later, and head up to the main house.

The next hour is a bustle of activity with me on the phone, Archer on his laptop, searching for the next available flight out of anywhere near us in New York to LA.

"There's nothing until Thursday."

"I wish we could get to her sooner." I bite my lip with worry.

His gaze is speculative. "You know who has his own plane?"

I stare at him. "No. You don't mean—"

He smiles and picks up his phone, putting it on speaker.

Oliver answers after one ring. "It's late." His voice is monotone.

"I know you're still working. I need a favor."

"What is it with you guys and favors?" I muse, keeping my voice quiet so only Archer can hear me.

"What is it?"

"Can I borrow your plane? I need to get to LA, preferably tomorrow."

"Not happening."

Archer lifts his brows at me, then says, "We need to go get Piper Fox and bring her back here. It's sort of an emergency."

"When?" His voice is clipped.

"Where do you keep your plane stored?"

"Teterboro."

"We can meet you there in the morning. Eight o'clock."

"Fine."

He hangs up.

I blink at Archer. "That was easier than I thought."

"I know how to handle Oliver because I understand how his thoughts work. He's very single-minded when he wants something."

He keeps talking about Oliver, but I can't focus on the words, I hear them, but they aren't registering.

I stare at him while he speaks, all the stress from the last couple of hours leeching out of me. He's so hot with his shirt half unbuttoned, his hair disheveled from earlier when I had my hands in it.

I move toward him, pushing him back on the couch. "I have single-minded focus sometimes too."

"Do you?" His grin is infectious.

We move together, yanking off clothes, attacking each other with eager concentration.

I can't believe this is my life right now.

I stare at the steps leading up to the sleek white plane.

My sworn nemesis is using his private jet to fly us to LA to rescue my little sister.

We were greeted at a private terminal and then driven straight onto the tarmac.

My mouth pops open when we head up the stairs and the pilot greets us. She has sleek blond hair pulled back into a bob and bright-red lipstick. "Welcome aboard," she says, shaking our hands as we enter the plane.

"Thank you."

We move further inside. It's all golden and bright. There are sleek cream leather seats toward the middle with shiny wood desks. A sofa lines one side. In the back, steps lead into another room of some sort. Not much of it is visible from where we're standing near the front.

Sitting in one of the seats, a laptop open in front of him, is the man I've been warring with for months now: Oliver Nichols.

"Oliver, this is Finley Fox. Finley, this is Oliver Nichols."

Oliver isn't quite how I pictured him. I imagined some kind of blond Adonis with a chiseled jawline. Oliver isn't quite the giant I had worked up in my imagination. He's more like a swimmer or a runner, sleek and trim, but his presence somehow takes up the whole damn plane anyway. He has dark hair and a probing gaze, and he's dressed in a navy-blue suit and tie.

Archer and I are a lot less formal. I opted for jeans and layers—a tank top, T-shirt, and jacket—since it will be much warmer on the West Coast.

"Finley." Oliver nods and shakes my hand, his grip firm but not hard.

"Thank you for your help with all of this," I tell him.

"It's not entirely altruistic. I appreciate her work, and I've been wanting to meet her for a while now. Make yourselves at home. If you need to use the facilities before takeoff, they're in the rear." He gestures behind us to the next room.

I nod. "I'll do that now." Curiosity compels me to check out the rest of the plane. This might be my only chance to fly on a private jet, so I'm not missing any opportunities to explore.

I leave my small overnight bag with Archer and make my way to the back of the plane, heading up the two steps and through the doorway into . . . it's a bedroom. My mouth pops open again. It has a queen-size bed covered in a dark-red comforter that makes me want to fall on top of it and take a nap.

The bathroom is through another narrow door, and I make my way inside, barely holding in my gasp.

This is not your normal airplane bathroom in which your knees hit the door when you sit down and there's barely room to wipe.

It's almost as big as my bathroom back home. There's a full-size shower and tub, all sparkling clean and gleaming white. The counters look like marble. Is that even possible? I knock on the material, frowning.

It's almost too pretty to pee in.

But I don't want to dawdle too much, so I finish up my business and make my way back out to the front, where Archer sits on the sofa, talking to the flight attendant.

"Can I get you something to eat or drink? We have a lovely frittata and coffee or mimosas." The flight attendant is the prettiest man I've ever seen. He has a low, soothing voice and an elegant manner that puts me immediately at ease.

"Get me the lobster frittata and coffee with cream. No sugar," Oliver yells from his seat.

I wince.

"Coffee would be great, Will." I read the gold-plated name tag on his lapel.

Poor Will stares in Oliver's direction, offers me a shaky smile and then bolts for the front of the plane to the little kitchen.

"Have you ever been on Oliver's plane before?" I ask Archer, tugging my jacket off.

He shakes his head. "Never had cause to beg use of it. Hadn't needed any favors from Oliver before now, not like this."

"You never told me what was up with the favor thing. You came to the cottages because you owed Oliver, he's doing this because he owes you . . . and Mason. You said you were calling in a favor. How did Oliver owe you if you already owed him?"

The corner of his mouth tips up. "It's a thing we do. We all owe each other, so if one of us calls in a favor, we're duty bound to honor it. There's no limit, but we can only use them on things that are really important."

"Why isn't there a limit?"

He considers the question. "Is there a limit to what you would do or wouldn't do for any of your family?"

"Of course not."

He nods. "We don't have family. We only have each other. So this is something we can do. We don't really know how to act like actual family. We don't see each other at holidays. None of us would know what to do with ourselves or even how to initiate something like that. We barely see each other in person. But we can do this. This we understand."

I glance over my shoulder at Oliver as the plane moves slowly down the runway, preparing for takeoff. He's opened his laptop, working, ignoring us.

My heart breaks for Archer and Mason and a little for Oliver too.

"Where's my coffee?" Oliver yells.

But he's still a total ass.

Archer

I call Mason as soon as we land.

He procured a room for Piper at the Ritz-Carlton in Marina del Rey, which is only five miles away from the airport. He returned this morning to meet us all there.

"They're already in the lobby. They just ate breakfast," I tell Finley as we slide into Oliver's limo only minutes after landing.

It's only ten in the morning LA time.

"I'm so glad Mason was able to get to her. Tell me more about him." She turns to me. "You met him at camp too, right?"

"Yes. Now he owns a few gyms here in LA and teaches self-defense and various martial arts classes."

"Wow. You guys turned into quite the success stories."

"Yes, yes, we dug ourselves out of poverty to become the thriving men you see before you." Oliver leans back, adjusting his suit jacket. "It's all very Disney Princess. Can we talk about something else?"

"Like what?" Finley asks him.

His eyes are speculative. "This boyfriend, Ben?"

Finley nods.

"He was also her manager, correct?"

"Yes."

"Will she be requiring new representation now that he is apparently no longer in the picture?"

She shrugs. "I think so, but I don't know how any of that works. You'd have to talk to Piper about it."

His lips purse, and he nods.

Finley leans back in the seat, her gaze drifting to the streets and palm trees flying by.

I take her hand and put it in my lap.

Within minutes, we're pulling up at the hotel. My shoes squeak against the marble floor, and I hear voices echoing around the lavish lobby.

We find Mason and Piper sitting on a plush purple sofa smack in the center under a sparkling chandelier glittering in the bright morning light. Other guests mill about the area, heading to the attached restaurant or checking in at the counter.

Piper and Finley hug. Oliver and I shake Mason's hand in greeting.

"This is Archer and Oliver," Finley introduces us.

We shake hands. Her grip is delicate, but her hands are calloused—an artist's hands.

Piper is petite, like Finley, but more fine-boned. Finley is a hawk, and Piper is more like a hummingbird.

I clap Mason on the back. "Thanks for everything."

"Of course." He flashes me a bright smile.

"I own one of your pieces," Oliver says to Piper.

She's holding on to Finley's arm, her face wan, eyes smudged with gray. Her brows lift at his statement. "You do? Which one?"

He never mentioned anything about this to me, only that he wanted some of her pieces for a show, not that he owned any of them. When did he obtain it?

Finley gives me a questioning look, and she must be thinking something similar. I shake my head slightly.

"*Lamentation*," Oliver answers.

"That's one of your earlier pieces, isn't it?" Finley asks.

Piper nods.

"Who do I need to contact to acquire more of your work?"

"Is now the best time for this conversation?" Finley glares at Oliver, but his gaze is still focused on Piper.

She swallows, shifting on her feet. "I'm not sure right now. I'll have to get back to you."

Oliver purses his lips then nods. "Fine." He looks

her over. "Do you have a bag? Archer mentioned we may have to pick up some of your possessions."

Her response is low. "I don't have anything. I had to leave suddenly."

"Well then. Let's go."

She shakes her head. "I'd rather not. Ben is probably there. He'll make things . . . difficult." Her grip on Finley's arm tightens.

"Nonsense. There is one Ben and five of us."

"No." Piper swallows, turning pleading eyes to Finley. "I can't do it. I can't see him. What if he makes me stay?"

Oliver's scowl deepens. "He will do nothing of the sort. You won't have to see him. We can take him out, and then you can go in to gather your personal effects."

I step into the discussion. "Between the three of us, we won't have any issues getting him to leave so you can get your things. I promise you this. You don't even have to see him. We can get him out while you wait in the limo. We'll keep you safe."

After a few long seconds, her chin lifts, and the family resemblance is apparent in the stubborn set of her jaw. "Fine. Let's do it."

Thirty minutes later, we're pulling up in front of her house, Mason following us in his black Camaro.

"Mason should stay with them and help get the items into the limo. We can take Ben out and down the street." Oliver's hand is on the door handle.

"Mason might take issue with that. He wanted an opportunity to have a conversation with Ben."

"He'll live."

Oliver gets out without waiting for anyone to agree with his plan.

"He's bossy." Piper watches him leave.

I put my hand on Finley's knee, shifting to follow him. "He's used to getting what he wants."

Finley squeezes my hand. "I'll call you when it's done."

"I'll make sure we leave the front door unlocked." I kiss her quickly on the lips before getting out of the car.

Oliver is already striding up the walkway toward the door.

Mason parks behind us.

I wait at the door until he reaches me. "Will you stay with them and help Piper get her things? We'll take him down the block somewhere."

Mason nods after a slight hesitation and gets in the limo. "You got it. Just make sure you get one in for me."

"You got it." I hurry after Oliver. He's already knocking.

The second the door opens, Oliver reaches for Ben. "Come with me."

"Excuse me? Who are you?"

"Someone who can make your life extremely diffi-cult if you don't listen." Oliver definitely has a way of infusing his voice with authority.

"I don't have to—"

Without waiting for him to finish, Oliver grabs him, twisting his arm against his back and putting him in a hammerlock, pushed up against the wall of the house.

"Yes, you do have to." He leans in to growl into his ear. "If you don't cooperate, not only will I break your arm, I'll alert the authorities and the press about how you've been treating Miss Fox. I have friends in higher places than you've ever dreamed. Do you understand?"

Like most bullies, Ben capitulates when confronted by a stronger opposition. I don't have to do anything but stand there, my arms crossed, keeping my expression blank and hard—which isn't difficult after what he's done to Piper.

Oliver lets him go, but Ben keeps glancing over at me as if he's waiting for me to strike.

"Can you walk on your own, or do we need to carry you?" Oliver takes a step toward him.

Ben flinches. "I can walk."

Oliver adjusts his suit sleeves. "Very good. I'll let you lead us to the next block, where we will stay until Miss Fox has had the opportunity to gather her possessions."

Ben hesitates, his eyes darting between us in bewilderment. "Who are you guys?"

"Irrelevant," I say, my voice low and menacing.

Ben cooperates, but he stares at the limo as we pass and then continues to glance behind him as we move down the tree-lined residential block, past Craftsman- and cottage-style houses.

"Keep your eyes in front of you," Oliver says.

At the corner, Ben stops and turns to face us, his features contorted with anger. "Who are you? What is she to you?"

Oliver stares at him, expression blank. "You don't need to worry about it. Turn around."

Ben laughs bitterly, shaking his head in disgust. "Is she fucking both of you? Trust me. She's not worth it. She's a lousy lay."

The movement is so fast, Ben's head snaps back and he hits the ground before I've registered that Oliver punched him.

Ben moans, rolling on his back in the middle of the sidewalk, clutching his jaw. "I'll sue you," he yells, bloody spit flying from his mouth.

Oliver, unruffled, shakes out his hand and then crouches, resting his elbows on his knees. He waits until Ben stops his groaning and meets his eyes. "I have more lawyers than you have teeth. Try it."

Twenty~Seven

Archer

Finley texts me the all-clear, and we walk Ben home, making sure he's inside before meeting them over on the next block, not wanting Piper to have to see him again even if he can't see her.

We say goodbye to Mason, who has to get back to work. Oliver and I shake his hand, but Finley and Piper take turns giving him giant hugs.

Finley says something to him as I'm getting into the limo, something that makes him grin, his entire face lighting up with the motion.

I'll have to ask her what that's all about later.

"Were you able to get everything you needed?" I ask Piper as we're heading back toward the airport.

She nods. "At least the most important things: my

purse and phone, and a lot of my clothing and jewelry."

"What about your art?" Oliver asks.

A crease forms between her brows, her lips pressing together. "We found a few of the smaller pieces, a pocket watch, some hand-size animal sculptures I made a while ago, but the larger ones and the pieces I had been working on are gone."

Oliver frowns, leaning back in the black leather seat and tapping his finger on the armrest in the door.

By the time we're back on the plane, getting ready for takeoff, it's late afternoon. We're all relatively quiet and subdued—it's been a long day for everyone.

Oliver takes the same chair as before, toward the back. Piper, Finley, and I sit together on a long couch on one side of the plane.

Oliver has always set himself apart. Our seating arrangements aren't surprising. But after takeoff, instead of sitting alone the whole time, ignoring everyone while he works, Oliver moves closer, sitting on the couch across from us.

I stare at him, brows lifted.

He ignores my questioning look.

Once we're airborne, Piper gestures to him. "What happened to your hand?"

His knuckles are bloody. "Ran into something," he says.

I grin. He sure did. Even Finley chuckles before leaning into me and resting her head on my shoulder.

"Do you have a first aid kit?" Piper's gaze is trained on him.

He doesn't answer for a long minute.

"There might be one in the bathroom," I tell her when it's clear Oliver doesn't intend to respond.

She gets up, returns with the small red box a few seconds later, and sits next to Oliver.

She pulls out an antiseptic wipe and cleans his hand. They talk, but their voices are too low and the hum of the engine is too loud for me to overhear any of it.

Her movements are perfunctory and quick. As soon as she's done, she puts the kit away and returns to her seat beside Finley.

I lean my head back, enjoying Finley's weight pressed against my side. I start to fall asleep but wake up when Finley speaks.

"She's not for you."

I blink my eyes open. Finley is staring at Oliver, her jaw set.

His gaze is on Piper, who is lying down on the other side of Finley. She's curled up, sleeping, tucked against the arm of the couch.

"I know," he says, the words barely audible.

I shut my eyes again.

Then Oliver speaks. "I'll share the property, but since I'll be handling the renovations and general upkeep, I want a controlling interest. Fifty-one percent is more than reasonable."

Finley tenses against my side. "It's my home. I want the fifty-one percent."

Oliver is quiet, inscrutable. "It appears we're at an impasse, then."

Finley shrugs. "So it would seem."

Oliver's always had a good poker face, his expression like stone. "I'll give you the one percent if she does a show in my new gallery." He inclines his head. "I think that's more than fair."

She huffs out a frustrated breath. "I can't decide that for her—"

"I'll do it."

Piper is still lying down, curved against the couch, but her eyes are open.

Finley is already shaking her head. "Piper, you don't have to."

"I'll do it, I said." She looks at Oliver. "But I need time."

"I'll give you two months."

She sighs. "You know nothing about art. Smaller pieces might take me a few days or weeks, but it depends on too many factors. Do you want originals? Commissioned pieces? Depending on how large some of them are, the number of pieces required, not to mention the size of the gallery, I might need a year."

"Six months. And—" he hesitates, his eyes tightening, his mouth firming for a second before he continues "—you don't have to fill the gallery completely. As long as we have a few good pieces to showcase, we have other artists that can supplement. But your pieces will receive main positioning."

They stare at each other across the plane. Finally, Piper relents. "Fine."

Finley raises a hand. "And we name it Camp Aria."

His head tilts in assent. "Camp Aria it is."

I tug on Finley's sleeve, and we share a grin.

～

It's almost midnight by the time we make it back to the airstrip in New Jersey.

"It's late. You are welcome to stay in my building if you would rather drive back to Whitby in the morning." Oliver is casual, making the offer once we're off the plane and getting into the car that will take us to the lot where I parked my rental.

I'm too shocked to respond for a few long seconds. I've come to New York dozens of times over the years, and he's never extended an invitation. Those types of social graces are not in his wheelhouse. What is going on with him? And does it have anything to do with Piper?

"No, but thank you," Finley answers for us. "I want to get home and sleep in my own bed, even if it means a couple more hours of driving."

He nods and gets into his limo before we can do more than offer a hasty goodbye.

Piper sleeps the entire drive. Finley helps me stay

awake by brainstorming ideas for the new kids' camp and talking about how late we're going to sleep in tomorrow.

By the time we get home, we barely have the strength to climb up the stairs, pull off our outerwear, and fall into bed in a tangled pile of limbs and exhaustion.

I come to awareness bit by bit. The sun is shining through the thin curtains, casting a glow over the room and the woman in my arms. We're spooning, my body surrounding hers, my arm resting over her waist.

Her head twists toward me. "Archer?" her voice is low and sleepy.

I hold her a little tighter. "I'm here."

She shifts, turning around to face me, her eyes still closed. "Oh, good. Any new disasters I should be aware of?"

I chuckle and kiss the furrow in her forehead. "Not that I'm aware of."

She snuggles into me further, yawning against my chest. "Small miracles."

I rub her back.

She pulls away, blinking sleepily up at me. "What if you were to stay here permanently?"

My mouth pops open in surprise.

She swallows and keeps speaking. "I mean for good. I know we talked a little about it, and you said you'd stay, but I want it to be for more than a while. I already invited Mason over for Easter next month, and if you aren't here, that might be real weird."

Delight fills my chest, my heart expanding with lightness. "You invited Mason here for Easter?"

"Yeah. He seemed really stoked about it too."

"Is that what you were talking to him about when we were saying goodbye?"

She nods. "I'm going to invite Oliver too, even though he's a weirdo." Her nose wrinkles, and then she sighs. "I guess he's our weirdo now. You know, I thought my family was messed up, but yours is worse, I think. At least Oliver is. Mason seems cool."

I swallow back a lump of emotion building in my throat.

Her hands slide up, cupping my cheeks in her palms. "Get rid of your condo in Dallas, close your storage shed, and bring all your stuff here." She searches my face. "Make this your home."

"Finley." I duck my head to get closer. "You are my home. I love you."

She grips me harder, pressing her mouth to mine in a quick, hard kiss before pulling back with a sniff. "I love you too." Her smile is bright and wide and shoots an arrow of delight straight through my chest.

I tug her knee up over my thigh to get even closer.

She traces a finger over my jaw. "Are you sure it doesn't bother you that I have more baggage than a luggage factory?"

I rub my nose against hers. "We all have baggage, Fin."

"Some more than most. I still have healing to do."

"We're all a little tattered and torn. It's okay to not know, to not have all the answers." I hesitate. "And you're not the only one. I've been alone for so long, I don't even know how to be a part of a couple, let alone a family. I might make mistakes."

She cups the side of my face in her hand. "Something tells me you'll do just fine, but I know what you mean. Life is messy. It can't be tied up in a neat little bow. We can't control everything. But we can enjoy the time we have now with the people we love most."

"So wise." I trail a finger down to the edge of her tank top. "I can think of a really good way to enjoy some of this time we have."

Her chuckle is low, and her breath hitches when I slip under her bra. "That's the best idea you've ever had."

Then I proceed to show her just how enjoyable the rest of our lives will be.

Epilogue

One month later

"You can't mix the colors. That's cheating." Mindy frowns over at Oliver, who's sitting on the opposite side of the dining table.

I rip open a package of blue dye and pour it into a little plastic cup. "It's not a competition. How can it be cheating?"

Mason lifts his egg partway out of the container in front of him with the little tin scooper, checking the bright-pink color. "Besides, mixing the colors makes them ugly, so if it is a competition, he's losing."

"It's not ugly, it's unique." Oliver pours a little purple into a cup filled with orange liquid and stirs it. "You simply have pedestrian tastes."

Everyone is sitting around the dining table, which is completely covered with little cups of dye, decorating tools, and about a hundred hard-boiled eggs. It would be perfect if Jacob were here. And if Taylor and Mindy were on speaking terms . . . and maybe if Piper didn't look so exhausted, her skin tight with fatigue.

Mindy wrinkles her nose. "Okay, then it's gross. No one wants an ugly brownish-reddish-greenish-purplish egg or whatever."

"I like the ugly ones." Piper drops a yellow egg into a red-colored cup.

Mindy rolls her eyes heavenward. "You would."

My eyes stay trained on Piper. Is she getting thinner? Her cheekbones are more pronounced than they were just a few weeks ago.

"Does anyone need more eggs?" Taylor pops her head in from the kitchen, where she and Jess, Nora's wife, have been doing all the boiling, which is really just an excuse for Taylor to avoid being in the same room as Mindy.

"I think we're good." I gesture to the jam-packed table.

"Will you pass me the carton?" Nora asks me.

I hand her a dozen eggs from the stack in front of me. "Who is going to eat all these eggs?"

"We can make egg salad sandwiches for the crew," Archer suggests.

We've had a staff of a dozen workers coming and going over the past few weeks: engineers, contractors, and architects surveying the property and helping to plan the rebuild.

I lean into him. "Such a problem solver." I tip my head up, and he brushes his lips against mine.

"Gross. I will throw this at you." Mindy holds up a blue egg.

"It would be worth it." Archer squeezes my leg under the table.

Oliver catches my eye from across the table and offers a curt nod before returning his attention to his egg.

I hold back a laugh. He's not so bad really. Certainly not the devil of New York that I thought he was. He is all bark but very little bite—unless you're Ben, I guess. He might even have a soft, gooey center under all that bossy, overbearing exterior. He's been here every weekend since we made our agreement, and he has good vision, I'll give him that much.

Camp Aria is going to be amazing.

I have a little residual guilt for sniping at him that Piper wasn't for him. His response was so . . . lonely. It reminds me of his background, of what he must have gone through as a child.

It's not my place to decide who Piper dates. Not that it matters. I might have misread the whole thing. He barely looks at her. This is the first time they've been in the same room together since we got back, as far as I know. Maybe because of my harsh words?

Archer told me that I probably didn't need to

worry. Oliver doesn't really do romantic entanglements, for a variety of reasons. Most women want him for his money, he's had some issues with stalkers, and besides all that, he's never been able to relate well to people—romantically or otherwise.

Oliver takes his egg out of a cup that now appears black and plops it into a red one. "I don't understand the purpose of this activity. Seems like a waste of food."

The entire table erupts into a debate.

"It's a Persian tradition," Mason says.

"Yeah, it started in Mesopotamia and was adopted by Christians or something," Archer puts in.

"Eggs symbolize rebirth," Taylor yells from the kitchen.

Mindy makes a face. "And death. I think they're gross. Unless it's eggs Benedict or deviled eggs."

"I think they found fragments of decorated ostrich eggs in Africa dating back more than sixty thousand years," Nora says.

Piper stands up suddenly, and conversation screeches to a halt. "I'll . . . be right back. Just need some fresh air."

"Are you okay?" I ask.

"Fine." She smiles, but it's small and tight.

There's a slight hesitation, and then Mindy speaks, distracting the table while Piper escapes. "There's a restaurant in Le Parker Meridien that sells the most expensive omelet in the world. A thousand bucks, can you believe that?"

"It's a frittata." Oliver's eyes follow Piper as she exits through the kitchen, heading to the side door. "And it's stuffed with an entire lobster and topped with sevruga caviar."

The conversation veers to food, and after a minute, Oliver stands and excuses himself, following Piper.

Weird. He's been avoiding her. Is he going after her to badger her about her art?

I bite my lip. Should I follow?

Before I can turn the thought into action, Mindy stands up and goes after Oliver.

Archer and I exchange a glance, wordless communication passing between us.

Hours later, after the painted eggs have been dyed and admired, peeled, and turned into egg salad for the crew next week, after everybody has settled in for their own entertainments, Piper finally comes to me to talk.

Archer and I are in the office, putting together my new desk, and we are trying to decipher instructions that look like English but may be some alien tongue that morphs and transforms as the reader reads.

Piper finds us there among scattered table legs and nuts and bolts. "Hey, Fin, can I talk to you for a second?"

"Of course." I glance at Archer, who is already rising to his feet.

"I'll take these out to Oliver and see if they make

more sense to him than me." Archer squeezes my arm as he passes into the house and shuts the door behind him.

"I'm going to New York," Piper says once we're alone.

I stand up. "Did Oliver put you up to it?"

She crosses her arms over her chest. "No. Well, sort of. But don't worry, I'm going to stay with Mindy."

"What do you mean 'sort of'?"

"I haven't been able to create anything." She swallows. "Not for a while. What I was making with Ben was . . . it wasn't the same."

"Oh. Piper." I move toward her, giving her a hug.

Her art is everything to her. More than mere self-expression. After the loss of Aria and Dad, she released all of her grief and frustration into her pieces. One of her first major sales was a sculpture of a woman, wrapped in a blanket, screaming. It was called *Despair*. It still amazes me that she somehow made the metal look soft and liquid, the woman's face barely perceivable between the folds of the blanket surrounding her.

She sniffs against my shoulder. "I love it here. It's home, but it's hard too."

I pull back to look at her. "Is it because I'm too smothering?"

"No." She chuckles, wiping at her eyes with the back of her hand. "I've been enjoying the coddling, actually. But I could use a change of scenery. I think about Aria and Dad too much, see them around every corner, you know?"

I rub her shoulder. "I do. That's hard. I'm sorry."

She shrugs. "It will be good for me. I need to get out there. New York is an inspiring city. Maybe it will shake something lose, help me move on so I can create again and not be so . . . stuck."

"On Ben?"

She lifts a shoulder. "Yes. Not him, personally, because I'm over him. He was such an asshole, but I need to move on from . . ." She lifts a hand, unable to find the words.

"From the way he treated you?" I ask softly.

"Yes. That." She nods. "And you should be nicer to Oliver. He's not a bad guy."

My mouth pops open. "What do you mean? I am nice. I've been playing nice when we work together, and I invited him for Easter."

She smiles, a real smile, not the tight expression she's been wearing like a mask for the past month.

I narrow my gaze on her. "Was this his idea? You going to New York?"

"Sort of." One side of her mouth quirks up. "He offered to let me stay in his building."

My eyes fly heavenward. "A building? He would have a whole freaking building to live in. Couldn't he just have a penthouse or something like all the other rich assholes in New York?"

Her smile broadens. "Mindy offered me her spare

room, rescuing me from the terrible fate of living in a mansion with servants."

I laugh. "Not to mention the devil himself."

"He's not a devil. I know the devil, Fin, and Oliver is not him." She lays her hand on my arm, soft and light, a butterfly touch. "But I'm sorry to leave you and Archer, even though you probably want some alone time. These walls are thin." She wrinkles her nose, her brows lifting.

"Yikes." I put a hand over my eyes, face heating with thoughts of what she might have heard. "Sorry."

"No. Don't be sorry. I'm happy you're happy. Archer is genuinely a wonderful person." She smiles, but it's small and sad.

"Do you want to talk about what happened with Ben?"

She sighs. "Not yet. I don't want to burden you."

"It's not a burden. We're family. Sometimes you have to let things out. You don't even know what might be in there, dragging you down."

"I will. I promise. I just need a little more time to . . . I don't know, sort it out myself."

Later, when the guests have gone to their rooms, Archer and I are snuggled together, as we are every night, downloading the events of the day.

This has become our nightly routine—wrapped up together, sharing whispered words and secrets, a dialogue that generally culminates in a more vigorous activity.

"Today was a good day," he says.

"It was." I don't mention my continuing worries about Jacob or Mindy and Taylor or Piper's struggles. We already talked about all of that, and he's right. It was a good day despite everything.

I had *almost* my whole family together for the first time in more than a year. Maybe in another year or sooner, it can be complete.

He presses his lips to my forehead. "It's only going to get better."

When Archer says it, I almost believe it.

Coming up next is Piper and Oliver's story: *The Fox and the Rebound*. Scheduled for release fall 2022. Preorder available now!

Want a little more Oliver prior to the events of this story? Check out book six in the Imperfect Series: *Imperfectly Delicious*.

Go here to sign up for the newsletter! www.authormaryframe.com

Mary Frame is a full time mother and wife with a full time job. She has no idea how she manages to write novels, but it probably helps that she's a dedicated introvert. She doesn't enjoy writing about herself in third person, but she does enjoy reading, writing, dancing, and damaging the ear drums of her co-workers when she randomly decides to sing to them.

She lives in Reno, Nevada with her husband, two children, and a border collie named Stella.

She LOVES hearing from readers and will not only respond but likely begin stalking them while tossing out hearts and flowers and rainbows! If that doesn't creep you out, e-mail her at: maryframeauthor@gmail.com

Coming 2022 a brand new Small Town Rom Com Family Series:

Between a Fox and a Hard Place

The Fox and the Rebound

9 781954 372146